Gem of a Lady

Keisha Lapsley

Gem of a Lady

Copyright © 2020 by Keisha Lapsley

This book is a work of fiction. The characters, locales, incidents, or persons portrayed in are fictitious. Any similarity to real persons, living or dead, is purely coincidental and not intended by the author. This is a product of the author's imagination.

For ordering, booking, permission, or questions, contact the author please visit www.authorklap.com or email at keycitypro@gmail.com

Publisher: KeyCity Publishing

Cover Design:

ISBN 9780999531464

Table of Contents

Stephanie's Monologue

Ugh!!!! I want to scream, but somehow, I can't; nobody will hear me, and half the time, I don't think no one even cares. I carry everything because, apparently, I was chosen for this, but I don't know how to release it all. I've done it all. I want to help, but I can't seem to find the words. I long to reach out, but my compassion is too short. He asks me what I think, but he really doesn't want to hear what I think. His mouth invites, but his heart really doesn't want to listen to what I have to say.

The Holy Spirit tells me to keep quiet and to just listen, and I do, attentively, but now I'm in a funk because of it. I want to release, but I can't seem to let go. I'm so tired in my body, my mind, and in my spirit. I don't know what to do anymore. I've ministered all that I know how, but now there is nothing left to say. I guess this is what being a Proverbs 31 woman is about following the Spirit no matter what you feel. Waiting to exhale just isn't enough. It was suitable for a time, but it's not a lasting feeling or exercise because, by the time I exhale, it's time to inhale again. I love him with all my heart, all that's within me. It's like if I move left, I may tip the scale, and if I move right, I tip the scale too, so I guess I have to stand still and see the salvation of the Lord.

Have you ever been in a place where you are tired, and you are still asked to pray? It's draining, isn't it? Sometimes I don't have a prayer to pray. Sometimes I need prayer myself. I don't know what is going on. I thought I knew, but I can't even say that's it anymore. I am in the stages of "I don't know," and it's a path that I can't understand. I guess being a Proverbs 31 wife isn't always having a perfect life but managing well the life God gave you. It's about doing everything in your power to make sure your family is well and not just well-off. Hmmm…that's a thought. I always thought this woman was perfect with the perfect life, but it's not that. What makes her a virtuous woman is that she knows how to keep everything together when everything seems to be falling apart.

Now the story can begin…

Chapter One: Your Sin Will Find You

"Hello, my name is Ash, and I'm with "Lena," the talk show," she said introducing herself after Stephanie opened the door.

"Oh, yes, they did say you would be coming by today. I'm Stephanie Bennet…wait a minute, don't I know you? You look familiar," she asked.

"Uhm…no, I don't think so," Ashley said.

"I'm sure I'll remember, just give me some time. I'm good with faces. Anyway, how are you doing today?" said Stephanie.

"I'm good! May I come in?" Ash asked with her field of followers behind her.

"Oh, yes, I'm sorry. Please forgive me. I've just never done anything like this before," Stephanie said.

"That's alright. Many people get nervous at first. This is my crew, who will be in your home daily. This is Todd, Britney, Chelsey, Corey, Rodger, and our intern Tashell," Ash said.

"Nice meeting all of you," said Stephanie after shaking their hands.

"Is it okay if they look around while we talk? They need to see where the best place would be to set up," Ash asked.

"Of course. My husband is upstairs getting ready. Let me go get him, and we can get started," said Stephanie.

"Great," responded Ash.

Stephanie went upstairs and checked on her children and her husband.

"Grant, the people from the television show, is downstairs."

"Honey, are you sure you really want to do this?" Grant, her husband, asked.

"I had reservations about it before, but I'm okay with it now. I have a strong feeling like I'm supposed to do this," she said.

"Okay, just making sure," he said.

"I know this is a lot, but I have to trust the vision God gave me. However, you have to be willing to do it. Do you want me to do this?" she asked.

"You know I'm a private person, and this is totally out of character for me, but because you are sure about it, I am sure, but if things get too out of control, I will cut the show short. I'm not going to go for no foolishness. This is our life we are sharing, and I'm not going to lose you or my children for the sake of a dollar and a show," Grant said, clarifying his stance.

"I'm with you on that," Stephanie said.

"Have you checked on the children?" Grant asked.

"I passed by their rooms, but I will again on our way downstairs," she answered.

"I'm ready. What about you?" he said.

"As ready as I'll ever be," she replied.

They walked by their two-year-old daughter's room to see that she was still napping. Then they walked by their six-month-old baby daughter's room, who was fast asleep, and their five-year-old son's room. Stephanie and Grant walked downstairs to finish the final touches before the cameras started rolling. Stephanie walked up to Ash and said, "Ash, this is my husband…"

"Ashley?" Grant said.

"Hello Grant, nice to see you again," Ashley said in a shocked but familiar kind of way.

"Ashley? From the documentary?" Stephanie asked.

"Yes, that's her," Grant said, acting squeamish.

"I thought I knew you," Stephanie said.

"That was so long ago," Ashley said.

"I know right," Stephanie said. Grant squeezed his wife's hand tight. Stephanie asked him, "Grant, are you alright?"

He acted like he would answer but paused instead, and his wife asked again, "Grant, are you okay?"

"Uh…Uhm…yeah, I'm fine. Stephanie, can I talk to you for a minute?" Grant said as he pulled his wife away to talk secretly.

"What was that all about?" Stephanie asked.

"There is something I need to tell you," Grant urgently spoke.

"Don't say what I think you're going to say?" Stephanie said cautioning him.

"We are not going to be able to do this today."

"Why?"

"We need to talk."

"Talk about what? Grant, don't start with me! Whatever it is, you better spill it and spill it now before I really get mad."

"That's Ashley, the one who followed me around about the documentary. Babe, it's not good for her to be here."

"Why? Have you slept with her?"

"It happened three months after we got married."

"You what!"

"And I didn't end it until three months later."

Stephanie's heart fell to the floor, her eyes turned red, smoke came out of her ears, and fire was on her tongue, "You mean to tell me the first year of our marriage was based on a lie."

"No, it wasn't. I broke it off because I was feeling guilty about everything. I didn't like lying to you. I loved you, and I wasn't going to leave you for her, and I told her that. She was furious, and she vowed that she would get me back."

"I should mop the floor with you and that chick! You lyin' sack of…Jesus! Lawd, he gone bring the project girl up outta me! After all this time, you had me thinking I was the problem in our marriage when it was you too."

"I wanted to tell you a few times, but I didn't want to lose you."

"You kicked all that crap about what marriage and sex is supposed to be but turned around and did the exact opposite. I'm so over this." Stephanie walked away from Grant and into the room with the crew and said, Y'all have GOT to get up out my house. All y'all. Tell your producers that we are not doing this. Let them find someone else. I ain't talkin' on nobody's talk show ta-day!"

"Stephanie, I don't understand. Why are you doing this?" Ashley asked, acting surprised.

"Lil girl, if you don't get out of my face playing like you don't know what's going on, there will be a nationwide search for two legs, and a coochie cause you won't leave here with either one! Get out my house, and I suggest you take that first and final warning because I WON'T suggest it again," Stephanie declared.

"Stephanie, I'm sorry," Ashley said.

"Sorry, don't live here right now, but 187 Genuine Skull-dragging Street does," Stephanie said. Then Stephanie looked up at the ceiling, talking to herself but for everyone else to hear, "Lawd, it's the not leaving my house for me."

"I'm leaving, but before I do, can I say one thing?" Ashley asked as her crew watches this whole thing transpire.

"What is that?" Stephanie said, balling up her fists.

"That happened a long time ago. I'm married now. I don't want Grant. I'm over that and have been for years. I have my own children with a husband that I've been married to for years. I'm sorry that I had an affair with your husband. I was wrong, and rest assured that if you allow us to continue, I will not be any trouble," Ashley said.

Stephanie drew back her fist and went to swing, but Grant caught her fist before it landed. "No! What you need to be rest assured of is that THIS here is finished. It will not happen. Take ya cameras, ya crew, and step," Stephanie said.

Ashley and her camera crew left and did so quickly.

When the video clip ended, Stephanie turned back to the audience and the talk show host and said, "Lena, that's why I didn't do the show back then. My husband and I had to work out some things."

"Stephanie, could you tell our audience why you decided to do it after so many years when we come back from the commercial break?"

"Sure, I'd be happy to," Stephanie said.

"We are looking forward to it. We will return with our expert guest, Mrs. Stephanie Bennet, when we return. We will be right back. Stay with us," talk show host Lena Smith said to her audience.

After a few minutes of commercials, it was time to come back to the talk show, and the tech said, "5, 4, 3, 2…"

"We're back. We have with us today, Stephanie Bennet from the popular hit reality television show, "Gem of a Lady." The audience clapped, and Lena continued to say, "Before we went to commercial, I asked you to tell our audience why you decided to do the show now after so many years?"

"Lena, so many people have requested for my husband and me to do a season of the show, then the executive producer approached me, and I felt like my family, and I was ready. My husband and I worked out our issues, and there were no more surprises…well, at least on my end," Stephanie joked. Everyone was laughing, and Stephanie continued to say, "No, seriously, I realized back then, I had a lot of growing to do. One thing that I do not want to portray is a false image, and a bad witness for God, and had we done the show, then that is what would have been portrayed," Stephanie clarified.

"What do you mean by portraying a false image?" Lena asked.

"I wasn't going to pretend that I was this "gem of a lady" when I was anything but that. The show is based on women who live virtuously and know how to still be a gem despite things around her breaking down."

"But I thought the purpose of your show was to show women that we don't have to be perfect. I'm just saying that doesn't seem authentic. Don't we all deserve to be angry or upset when we go through things, though,

Stephanie? I mean, it's pretty unrealistic not to become upset when you have every right to."

"Absolutely, Lena, we all have a right. I'm not saying we are not allowed to become upset or angry; even God gets angry. It's an emotion that we have, but most of the time, we follow the scripture "be angry and sin not," but only the beginning part of it. It's the sin, not part, that gets all of us in a whole lot of trouble. And yes, our show's purpose is to let women know we don't have to be perfect, but it's also to show grown-woman status. So, yeah, we can be angry but can't fall into sin because of it."

"You're right about that," Lena responded and laughed along with the audience.

"That's where I fell short; I got angry and sinned. The show is about Christian women living the gospel example. I'm not saying that we are perfect on the show, and you'll see that in our upcoming web series, but an example has to be presented. Raise your hand or clap if you have children," Stephanie said to the audience. They did as she asked, and she continued to ask, "Do you tell them to be a leader and not a follower?" The audience clapped again. "Well, that's exactly what we are doing on the show. We are supposed to lead and not follow other detrimental examples that others have shown on other reality shows."

"Well said. But did I hear you say web series?" Lena responded.

"Yes, ma'am. Grant and I are doing a side web series to my show. It gives us room to be more creative and interactive. We're going to get deep into the problems of our marriage, what he did and what I did, and how to overcome it together," Stephanie clarified.

"I must say we need an example nowadays because so many people do wild and crazy things without thinking of the consequences later."

"If we want to change the world, we have to change ourselves first, and that's what most people forget."

"You also have a CD coming out."

"Yes, Lena, I do, but I just wrote the songs. Others sing them for me."

"Stephanie, why aren't you singing?"

"Lena, hun, you don't want that. I know my lane, and I'm not ashamed." The audience laughed so hard, even Lena's eyes were tearing up from laughing. "You are too funny," Lena said.

"I'm serious. Now, I'm not the worst singer, but I know that publicizing the noise I make at home just ain't right for the public's consumption," Stephanie said, giggling herself.

"Thank you for coming on the show. We pray that the CD is a success along with the web series and the show "Gem of a Lady." We look forward to seeing more from you," Lena said as the show's theme music began to play and end the show.

After being interviewed on the talk show, Stephanie went home to relax but quickly remembered that she was still "on TV" and geared herself up for that. She was glad that her time for the show was almost up. Each year they film a different family and her year was almost up.

It has been four years since the big blow-up from the first time the camera crew showed up at her house, and she found out about Grant's affair. They worked through it, but Stephanie made Grant feel the pain before she forgave. He didn't know how to handle his wife. He had never seen her like that before. Grant shed just as many tears as Stephanie did, and she made sure of it. By the time all of that was over, Grant never wanted to hurt his wife like that again.

After a few more months, the contract for the reality show ended. They were happy about it too because it was stressful being on camera all the time. The television executive producer wants them to do another season because of the ratings. Grant and Stephanie had fans and generated a lot of conversation and response. It's something they consider, but they aren't sure about it; all they know is for right now, they are done.

Chapter Two: Where It All Began

Grant and Stephanie were from different sides of the track. Grant grew up with the finer things in life while Stephanie was scraping the bottom of the barrel. Grant's parents were well off, and they gave him all the love he needed or at least how they thought they should love their son. He was the youngest of three children. He has two older brothers and a younger sister that's no longer with them. Grant wasn't the high school jock or even the most popular one. He was astute and into things that the "normal" teenager wasn't into; Grant is in love with science. He loves how things worked. That's what drove him to debate the Bible at first. He wasn't raised in the church, but he heard about God here and there. His love for science overshadowed anything miraculous. His parents had him and his brothers in private school. They didn't know about the other side of the tracks. Their parents kept it from them. They didn't mingle with the "commoners." They were working their way up to the "pie in the sky," and the "little folks" weren't going to stop them. Grant's love for science paid his way through college…where he met his match.

Stephanie was just the opposite of her husband. She was raised in a humbling environment. She was from the projects…nothing she was proud of but not what she rejected. Her mom and dad loved God but were some of the poorest people you would ever meet. They made the word poor say, "What! I'm not that poor." Either way, they didn't miss a church service. When the doors were open, they were there. When the doors were closed, they were the first ones there for whenever it opened. They were very well known in the community. Stephanie's father was the one people went to when they needed a calm person to help solve a situation. He'd always pray. Her mom was the one who would bring that "favorite" dish to any and all functions and events. She could cook her butt off and made sure that everyone was fed. No one went hungry around her, including her own. People didn't understand how she made that happen, but as long as she knew, that's all that mattered. Stephanie is the middle of five children. She has three brothers and one sister. They had their share of problems, but they came together as a family no matter what. This is what Stephanie remembers and tries to incorporate into her family on a daily basis. She worked hard in school. She was an average student. School just wasn't her thing, though she tried her best. Her love was cooking. She got an A in home economics all the time. It was one of the few A's she received on her report card. She didn't get accepted to a regular college. She was accepted into a culinary school. Stephanie always looked up to her mother and was forever in the kitchen with her whenever she cooked. Stephanie and her mother volunteer on the weekends at soup kitchens. She loves it! She hopes to open her own restaurant one day.

Grant and Stephanie saw each other the summer after her high school graduation. She and her friends were having fun on the strip one weekend...being teenagers. There was a big summer, expo celebration. They didn't know they stayed in the same city, and it's odd they never crossed paths. Stephanie was decked out in her lavender and white intermingling short summer dress with white-strapped sandals that curved her caramel brown legs, her hair cut in a bob with golden highlights and make-up to match the beauty that is her.

She was with her friends, and while they were walking about the expo and going to the different booths, there stood Grant, one tall drink of water. She could hardly take her eyes off him; that light brown-skinned, low-cut wavy-haired, baby face with a nice and freshly shaped mustache, wearing crisped pressed khaki slacks, a blue polo shirt and a gold bracelet (that by the way, drives Stephanie absolutely crazy; she loves men that wears a bracelet) and a gold necklace to match.

Grant caught the glance of the lovely young lady that was watching him. Oh, he was a ham, a lady's man. He would talk to potential clients about whatever it was he was selling and looking at her every chance he got. He winked at her one time to come over. She didn't care about what her girlfriends were talking about or what was going on at the time. All she cared about was whatever he was selling, she was going to buy…at all costs.

As soon as she walked up to him, a classy woman intervened. She was absolutely gorgeous and seemed to be his type. This woman had long hair (which obviously wasn't hers), long eyelashes (wasn't hers either), well-manicured nails (still wasn't hers), and feet, an outfit that screamed nine hundred dollars and shoes to match. She made it obvious they were together; hugged all up on him. Stephanie thought to herself, "Shoot, if you take away everything that isn't hers, this chicken head is me, and I'm the real thing. He must not like the "real" thing, and I ain't got no time for foolishness." He gave her a kiss on the cheek, and Stephanie walked off.

After that day, Stephanie couldn't get this man out of her head. He apparently was out of her league, but she didn't care. Even months later, he was still in her head. She couldn't forget his face. Little did she know; Grant couldn't stop thinking about her either. Something was intriguing about this woman he never met, who obviously isn't someone that he'd typically date nor who his parents would approve of for their son.

At that time, Grant was a college student in Miami, Florida, and Stephanie was going to attend culinary arts school in Albany, GA. She was away from home, Savannah, GA, and didn't like it much. She missed cooking with her mother in the kitchen. Stephanie was a girl that loved family and would stick close to home, but her love for cooking moved her away. She wasn't sure what God had planned for her life. As time went on, she forgot about the man with no name, and he went on dating "Ms. Glorification."

Just under a year passed, and the semester was wrapping up. Right before the end of the school year, Stephanie's college took a trip to Florida for a culinary cooking contest. She was the best student in her school, and they had high hopes for her. They entered her in the competition that a culinary school hosts every year, which her school tends to lose every year. They were hoping to end that losing streak now that Stephanie's in play. She was so stoked about this contest. It was all she could talk about to her parents. They couldn't make it to see her, of course, because they didn't have the money. Stephanie vowed one day she was going to make enough money to bring her parents out of the projects and shower them with the same love they gave her and gives to the neighborhood even until this day.

When they arrived in Florida, the other students wanted to go "out to play," but Stephanie was focused. She stayed in her room, studied, and practiced the dishes she was going to make. The contest was underway, and Stephanie was the forerunner. She made the other chefs mad because of all the love and accolades she received from the judges. Stephanie was very humble and even helped those who hated her. She gave them tips, and because of their hatred towards her, they didn't use the tips and lost. Stephanie was declared the winner and brought home the trophy. Her school finally won! They were all so excited. They went out to celebrate that evening before going back to Albany the next morning. They got to experience Miami in all its glory. The class went to the beach that evening and enjoyed themselves. Stephanie went up to the bar to order a soft drink. She was in a two-piece boy short swimsuit. It hugged her in all the right places. She wore her sunglasses and a big straw hat to hide her face from the sun. She looked almost glamorous herself.

While she waited on the bartender, one heck of a man strolled up, showing all that God gave him and in all His splendor. She wanted to "lay hands" on the chest that had a name written across it surrounded by a flower, but when she took the time to actually look up at the man's face, she recognized him. It was Grant. He walked up to her, and they began talking. She wasn't sure if he remembered her from over a year ago. She was waiting for "Ms. Glamorous" to walk up and steal her moment again. His game was tight, but Stephanie thought he was just a bit arrogant, which completely turned her off.

One thing Stephanie couldn't stand was arrogance. She hated it with a passion. She didn't like it nor hung around people who acted that way. Stephanie gave him the brush off and went back to have fun with her classmates. The girls thought she was crazy to let him go. All they could see was the looks, but Stephanie could have cared less about that. She just wasn't that type of chick. She realized her friends didn't know her as well as she thought they did.

On the other hand, Grant couldn't comprehend a female turning him down, "I mean, I'm Grant Bennet," he thought, but she could have cared less about "Grant Bennet." This drove him crazy. No one that he wanted ever turned him down. They waited on him to come to them because they knew better. This turned into a "hot pursuit" for him. He gave her his number and asked for hers, but she wouldn't give it to him and politely told him, "If I want to, I'll call you, and that's the only way you will get my number." He didn't know what to do with himself; not even high, Ms. Mighty treated him this way.

Stephanie went home with her classmates the next morning. They were still hyped about winning the trophy, and it also brought funds to their school. She called her parents and told them what happened and how she won the trophy. They were so proud of her. They knew she could do it. Her siblings were excited for her too.

It was almost time for her to go back home. The school was only for a year, and she would receive a certification. Soon enough, Stephanie would be home to cook in the kitchen again with her mother, and this time with some credentials behind her name. Her school connected her with a restaurant placement in Savannah, Ga, which was good news for her because she wanted to go home.

Meanwhile across state lines, Grant was doing well in college. He was top of his class, but one thing ailed him, his parents were getting a divorce, and science couldn't fix it; no kind of research could hold his parent's marriage together. The science Grant fiercely loved couldn't answer his questions of why. All he knew was going down the toilet and flushing fast; even his schoolwork became affected. He let his girlfriend of three years go, started hanging around a different crowd, and began questioning everything, even the very science he loved so much. Women around him now approached him, saying they are comforting him in his time of need, and he took advantage of it too. He slept around with different women and didn't care about how they felt. His parents were livid with him, well, at least his mother was because he reminded her of his father. They couldn't believe he let go of Tarina. Oh, they loved her and were hoping he would marry her, but Grant would have never asked her because he couldn't imagine himself with someone just as vain as him. He wasn't really into Tarina like that; she was convenient, making it even easier to break up with her. Grant was going into his third year of college, and it wasn't looking too bright.

Graduation time was upon Stephanie, and she couldn't be more thrilled. Her parents drove up to see their daughter walk across the stage. They knew Stephanie wasn't the scholar student out of all their children, not that she wasn't smart; school just wasn't her thing. However, she had a gift, and it was being cultivated with honors to prove it. "Cum Laude looks good on my baby," Mrs. Chase said. "Oh, stop crying, you big baby," Mr. Chase said, giggling. Stephanie walked across the stage with all smiles receiving her certification.

Stephanie returned home after graduation. On the way home, she felt a tugging to call Grant, even after all this time. She couldn't understand it. She finally called him after arriving home and unpacking her belongings. She had no clue why she was calling him because he disgusted her so. He answered the phone, "Hello," with a deep baritone voice. She started twitching in places she never let anybody "play" with, "Oh, this ain't nothing but the devil!" she thought to herself, hung up the phone, and slammed down on her bed quickly. Then Grant called her right back because he noticed that it wasn't a number he recognized. She let the phone ring and ring, so he hung up, eventually. Stephanie questioned why she was even calling him. Nothing about him screamed husband to her. He just looked good on paper or as a window display. She waited days before wondering if she should call him back. Stephanie couldn't understand why this was tugging at her. She was one who would pay attention to what God was trying to tell her, but she wasn't sure if this was him or not.

Two weeks passed, and Stephanie couldn't shake this feeling to call Grant. She gathered all the little nerves she had and called him again. This time when he answered, she actually spoke, "Hi, may I speak to Grant?"
"This is he. Who dis?"
"This is Stephanie."

"Stephanie, who?" Grant asked.

"It's been a while, but…," Stephanie began to say, but he cut her off.

"You are the girl from the beach! The one that gave me a hard time," he said.

"I gave YOU a hard time. Oh, you got to be kidding me. Have you listened to yourself lately?"

"What made you call after all this time?"

"I don't know."

"You called a few weeks ago too, didn't you?"

"Yes."

"Why did you hang up?"

"I can't tell you that."

"Why?"

"Just can't."

"What are you up to now?"

"I just finished school, and now I'm back at home with my parents."

"Finished? What kind of school you go to?"

"It was for culinary arts."

"Oh."

"How are you doing?"

"I'm alright."

"You don't sound like it."

"Got a lot on my mind."

"Like what, might I ask?"

"I don't want to talk about it."

"How about this, if you tell me what's on your mind, I will tell you why I hung up."

"You go first."

"No, you go first. I made the suggestion."

They both began to laugh nervously, but it broke the ice. Grant said, "My parent's divorce became final a few weeks ago. I just couldn't go back to school after that and moved back to Savannah…actually, all this happened right around the time you called and hung up on me."

This took Stephanie back because this was the reason God wanted her to call him, and on top of that, she wouldn't know what she would do if anything happened to her parents. Family means the world to Stephanie, and this is more than she could handle. Stephanie didn't know what to think because how could she minister to him about something she knows nothing about. She started praying on the inside…quietly. "I'm sorry, Grant. I don't know what to say."

"No one ever does. I just needed a shoulder to cry on," Grant said.

"I know it's late, but I can be that shoulder if you still need one."

"That's cool, but I'm kind of over it now."

"How did you get over it so fast?"

"Keeping my mind off of it."

"And how did you do that?"

"…didn't you say that you would tell me why you hung up the phone if I told you what happened to me?"

"Yes."

"So, what happened?"

"To be honest, I had no idea why I was calling you, but I did anyway, and…"

"What do you mean you didn't know why you were calling?"

"Grant, can I be honest?"

"By all means."

"You came off so arrogant like you were God's gift to women, and that is a huge turn off for me. That's why I didn't understand why I was calling you. Don't get me wrong, you are a very nice-looking man, but I can't stand arrogance."

"Well then, why did you call?"

"I can't honestly tell you."

"Alright, that still doesn't explain why you hung up."

"When I heard your voice, I started getting this strange feeling over me, so I hung up."

"I turn you on, huh Steph?"

"Steph…only my friends call me that."

"Can I be your friend?"

She paused then said, "Yes, I would like that."

"You didn't answer my question."

"What question was that?"

"I turn you on?"

"What does that mean?"

"You know what that means."

"Let's get something straight off the back. Ruby and I do not get into these types of conversations."

"Why? And who in the Batman's bat cave is Ruby?"

"Because I am a virgin and I am not going to have sex until marriage. Ruby is my jewel-friend."

"You can't be serious."

"Very."

"Well, what good is a jewel if no one ever sees it?"

"What good is a jewel that is accessible to everyone?"

"How old are you, grandma?"

"I'm not that old."

"I've never met a virgin before, or at least one that I couldn't tame."

"I have stood strong in the toughest of times."

"Man, you are going to be a challenge."

"A challenge that you will not win."

"You're right. I don't do that with friends anyway."

"That's good to hear."

That night, Grant and Stephanie talked for hours as if they had known each other since kindergarten. Neither one of them wanted to admit that they liked each other. Stephanie was different from any other woman that Grant dated before, and Grant was undoubtedly not Stephanie's type. She could see his game coming from a mile away, and it wasn't nothing she hadn't already heard.

For a long time, Grant and Stephanie maintained their friendship. She learned he was a science buff, and he found out she was a Christian, which really made him decide to keep it as a friendship. She encouraged Grant to return to school to finish his studies, especially since he only had less than two years left. He was more stable and wasn't distracted by his parent's problems anymore, so he returned to college. Stephanie's parents disapproved of their friendship. They didn't want their daughter falling for someone who didn't believe in God, and it was apparent Grant Bennett definitely had her heart. He was respectful towards her parents, though, and that won them over.

After a year, they could no longer avoid what was really going on between them. Stephanie's parents didn't like it. They kept pressuring her about dating someone not of the faith and how they were unequally yoked. They could see the heartache coming. Stephanie didn't care. She was head over hills in love with him. She stuck to her guns though about waiting to have sex until she is married. Grant never put her in any compromising positions either. He respected that she wanted to wait. Females couldn't believe Grant was being faithful to someone and especially to someone like Stephanie. She wasn't your typical "trophy" girlfriend. They were jealous and ticked off. They tried everything under the sun to break them up, but Grant wasn't having it. He laid down the law and told them to back off. He was in love with a lady, and her name was Stephanie.

Once they made their relationship official, they dated for two years, but it seemed like a sweet lifetime Now he's ready to pop the question. It was a rainy night, not storming but that light rain, the type of rain you love to watch from your windowsill. In his apartment, he put a chaise next to his window just for this occasion. He cooked a light dinner and had everything simple but presentable.

Earlier that day, Stephanie went to get her hair done for her date. Her beautician suggested an Italian wave sew-in. Stephanie thought about it and agreed. She thought she would try something different. It turned out so beautiful. She really liked the new look. She thought, "I could get used to this." Grant told her not to wear anything elegant because they were just going to be in his apartment. Therefore, she put on a pair of jean Capri's, a fitted shirt with sexy written across it with jewels on it that he gave her a few weeks ago. She was sharp and wasn't used to dressing like this, but she liked that look too. She put on some large hoop earrings and stilettos to match her outfit. Grant wore some jeans with ash down the front pants leg, a V-neck sweater vest with an undershirt to match. He had a preppy look going on.

Stephanie showed up at his door, and when he opened it, he just about fell to the floor and said, "You are going to have to go home and put on something else." Stephanie asked him, "Why do you say that?" He proceeded to tell her to remember how she felt when she called him for the very first time because that's how he was feeling. She laughed, pushed him to the side, and walked into the apartment, and said, "Boy, let me in with your silly self." He warned her. She loved his preppy look and was proud to go with her man anywhere. They talked for a while, but he couldn't get over how good his (hopefully) "future wife" looked. Grant put in a chick flick, turned off the lights, and sat dinner in front of them on his coffee table. She took her shoes off and got relaxed. After they finished eating, he popped some popcorn. Then as he sat the popcorn down on the coffee table, he nicely laid the ring box behind the bowl so when she picks it up, she will see the box. Grant was on pins and needles, waiting for the love of his life to pick up the bowl of popcorn. He could hardly stand it. After about twenty minutes, she finally picked up the bowl. Stephanie still did not notice the ring box until she put the bowl back down and spilled it because she put on the ring box. "Oh, I'm sorry, Grant," she said.

"It's okay, Steph. I'll clean it up."

"No, I did it, let me."

"Okay."

Stephanie turned on the lights and spotted something, "What's this?"

"Open it and find out," Grant said with great anticipation.

"OH MY GOD! This is beautiful."

"Stephanie, will you be my wife?"

"Grant, we never….I mean…oh my God."

"Please don't leave me in expectation."

"Grant…I'm sorry…I can't."

"What! What do you mean you can't?"

"Grant, you know we are very different."

"So."

"You don't believe in God."

"Stephanie, where did you think this would go? You've known that for as long as we've been friends. It doesn't matter to me that you believe. That's okay with me."

"But it's not okay with me."

"Why did you stay with me for so long? Why did you even get involved with me when you knew this about me?"

"I don't know. Honestly, I really didn't believe we would make it this far."

"Don't do this to me, Steph. I love you."

"I can't deny that I love you too, but..."

"Then marry me, Steph."

"I can't accept your ring, Grant. This night was perfect, but I'm sorry."

Stephanie ran out in tears. Grant was sad and confused from the rejection of his marriage proposal. He never thought for a second, she wouldn't accept his proposal. It was the furthest thing from his mind. He began to wonder what was so special about this God that would not allow her to marry him. Grant's heart was broken.

Neither one of them called each other for weeks, and he couldn't take it anymore, so he finally picked up his phone to call her. Stephanie didn't answer his call. She avoided his phone calls for a long time. A month passed, and still no Stephanie. Grant's friends tried to get him out of the house and kept telling him that they told him so about her. His best friend, Xavier, could see how hurt Grant was and tried everything to cheer him up. He saw how Stephanie changed him for the better. He knows Grant all too well, and this will not be good for him. Xavier told their mutual friends, "Y'all need to stop telling him how bad Stephanie is for him. That's not going to help. And getting up under another chick ain't gone help either. Let the man breathe." They left Grant alone, but once the females heard Grant was free, they were like Shrimp on the Barbie, caught, cooked, and ready to be consumed. They "knew" she was no good for him and were back to "comfort" Grant. Since Stephanie wasn't answering his phone calls, he fell back into his old ways. He longed for her, though. No amount of sex could equate with the love he had for Stephanie. Her parents were glad she said no, but their hearts broke to see their daughter in so much pain.

Stephanie got a new job working at the restaurant "Cove" and throwing herself into it. Every time they needed someone, she was there.

Four months passed by, and Grant decided to call Stephanie's father to see if they could talk. Stephanie's father, Mr. Chase, was glad to hear from Grant. They went to a basketball game and discussed Stephanie while they were there. At least the game could help at uncomfortable moments. Grant asked Mr. Chase what was so special about this God that kept breaking his heart.

"Son, it's not God that's breaking your heart. He's actually tugging on it."

"I believe in science, Mr. Chase."

"Yes, I know, but tell the truth, science has let you down."

"Yes, sir."

"There are some things that you can't explain."

"Yes, sir."

"I'm not going to tell you that you won't have disappointments in God, but in your disappointments, He will be the lifter of your head. Tell me, Grant, what does science have that God doesn't?"

"I'm not sure I understand your question."

"You understand."

"No, I really don't. How can I compare something against something that I don't believe in?"

"In science, you deal in theory, correct?"

"Yes, sir."

"In order to prove your theory, you have to compare what you believe in versus what you question, right?"

"Yes, sir."

"Well, that's the same thing that I'm asking of you."

"Okay. Science explains everything that happens, but from what I hear, the Bible only tells you what happened, and I need to know how. Science provides the how for me."

"If I give you an assignment, will you be willing to do it?"

"If it will bring Stephanie back to me, yes."

"No, that's the wrong answer. You have to do it because you want to do it."

"Alright."

"Here's the assignment. I want you to read the Bible starting at Proverbs and ask God to open your understanding. Ask Him to prove himself to you as you read."

"That's all?"

"Yes, and I will even get a Bible for you. I have plenty at home."

"Can I ask you another question, Mr. Chase?"

"Sure."

"I got the feeling you and Mrs. Chase did not approve of your daughter and me dating. Was I wrong?"

"No, you were right."

"But why? Haven't I always been respectful to both of you and Stephanie? Did I ever mistreat her? Did I ever disrespect her?"

"As long as I've known you, Grant, you've been respectful and have treated Stephanie very well, but I can't allow for good works to overshadow what the Bible says about being unequally yoked."

"Now, what does that mean?"

"Some of the most heated battles in marriage are because two people believe in something totally different from the other. Jesus is the only foundation there is and the only one that can be built upon without the whole house falling. If one's foundation is anything other than Jesus, his house is built upon sand instead of a rock."

"Okay, I can understand that to a point, but it's not proven to me yet."

"It's not my job to prove it to you. You're the scientist; prove me wrong. That's what you do, right?"

"Absolutely."

"But I will say this one last thing and leave you alone. Jesus' standards are different from the world's ways. How can you say you love someone when you don't love what is the very core of them?"

Grant was stunned at Mr. Chase's question. He had no comeback; not even a scientific theory could answer the question that Mr. Chase asked. They watched the basketball game and enjoyed one another's company. Mr. Chase gave Grant plenty to think about while he followed Mr. Chase home to get the Bible from him. Stephanie stayed in her room and wouldn't come out. Grant couldn't figure out how come she was so standoffish with him. As far as he knew, she was the one who owed him an explanation. He was ready to move forward in life with her. As he stood just one foot inside the apartment, he yelled, "I love you, Steph," grabbed the Bible from Mr. Chase, and walked out without even a response from her.

Be-it-unknown to Grant, Stephanie was dying inside without him. She loved him more than words could say, so much so that she was becoming sick. She wouldn't eat, could hardly sleep, and stayed to herself a lot. When she heard him yell that he loved her, Stephanie broke down in tears. She wept sore. She watched him through her window, but he didn't see her. Stephanie prayed about how come she couldn't marry the man she knows God has for her and all because of her "silly" standards. How could love do this to her? She desperately wanted to say yes to Grant's proposal, but in her heart of hearts, she knew it wasn't the right thing to do.

That very night, Grant went straight to work to prove Mr. Chase wrong. He was determined to win Stephanie's heart by proving what she believes isn't as strong as she thinks it is and how come it's keeping them apart.

As months went on, Grant didn't call Stephanie, didn't hound her or anything. He was on a dog hunt. Just when she thought she was over him; he shows up at her church one Sunday morning. Feelings rushed through her like a "rushing mighty wind." He sat in that church, snickering, and shaking his head at the pastor and what he was teaching. Grant had been reading the Bible and listening to what the pastor said made him that much more dislike God. He kept thinking to himself, "And this is why she won't marry me? He's not even teaching the Bible right." After service, he approached Stephanie and asked her, "Can we talk for just one minute?"

"Why can't you let this go, Grant? It's over."

"Just for one minute."

"Okay."

"Walk with me to my car, please."

"That's going to take more than a minute."

"Look, Steph…you owe me at least that. Hear what I have to say."

"Fine!"

As they walked to Grant's car, he asked her all kinds of questions like; how she's doing, what has she been up to, and the mother of all questions, why she won't speak to him. Her response was, "You said you wanted to talk, but if this is what you want to talk about, then I'm sorry, but I'm going to have to leave."

"Okay, Steph."

"Now, what is it that you want to say to me, Grant?"

"You say we are unequally yoked, and that's why you won't marry me, but your father gave me a challenge, and I've taken hold of it. I still have a problem with this "God" thing.

"And why is that?"

"I've been reading the Bible, and this morning I have listened to what your pastor had to say, and it did not line up with what I read."

"How would you know? Revelation has not been opened to you."

"Revelation? Look, I don't know much about revelation, but I have been learning about truth and today's message wasn't about that. It actually turned me off even more."

"I don't have to sit here and listen to this from someone that won't take the time to truly learn of God. You are a skeptic, and this is the main reason I won't marry you. We are having an argument in a church parking lot over what I believe and what you don't. Truth? You speak of something you know nothing about! You don't know about truth! You won't even let

God minister to you! You won't let Him in, and you expect me to let you in? You've got to be kidding!"

"Steph…I."

"…I don't want to hear it. When you truly love God, I will know, but until then, it would be best for us not to see each other again."

Stephanie walked off and left Grant in the parking lot, all alone, questioning, sad, and perplexed. The dog pound could have found him and locked him up because he looked just like a lost puppy. Walking off was the hardest thing Stephanie had to do, but she knew it was the right thing. Grant thought he had her, but this time he felt like he lost his last chance with her.

Grant went home with a lot to think about and wondering if Stephanie was even worth chasing anymore. He figured he could never come to terms with her, and he wasn't going to budge about his beliefs. "This is a losing battle," he thought.

Later that night, Grant had a dream, and in the dream, God said to him, "Don't lose heart. Stephanie will be your wife," and showed him getting married to Stephanie.

In the dream, Grant asked, "How? She doesn't love me anymore."

"She loves you, but you have to stop acting as if I don't exist when you know in your heart I do."

Grant woke up from the dream abruptly, and tears slowly falling down his face. He cried out, "I'm so mad at you! What kind of God allows these kinds of things to happen? You left me as a child, but you want me to believe in you as a man! I…I can't…"

Then the Lord spoke to Grant's heart, "I know it hurts. I know it does, but you can't blame me for that."

"I can, and I will."

"Your baby sister is dear to me too. It was time for her to come home to Me."

"But why? I prayed and prayed and prayed for You to save her life, and You didn't. You knew how close we were."

"There is a time to be born and a time to die. I know that doesn't make you feel any better, but I only kept Adrianna with you all for a short time to capture your hearts for a lifetime. When she died, it was right around the time you began to love science because science explains things, and you believe I don't. I have already explained everything in My word and my children…including you, you are still shocked when things happen in your life."

"Why didn't you come to me when I called?"

"I did, but you did not hear."

"Why didn't you heal my heart?"

"I tried, but you wouldn't let Me."

"Why did you let Adrianna die? She was only nine years old…and from something as simple as the flu? How could you?" Grant cried out.

"Money doesn't buy what you need. Science doesn't explain unexpected events; it only explains what has already happened. I am everything you think I'm not."

"Everything fell apart. My parents aren't even together anymore."

"Your parent's marriage was failing even before Adrianna's death."

"They were happy."

"Were they? Think about it. You do not see the bigger picture. Adrianna and everything you've been through draws you to Me even now."

Just then, a picture of Adrianna, Grant's sister, flashed in front of his eyes. It seemed as if she was right there in the room with them. Grant cried even more. He wept for hours and decided to forgive God for what he thought God did to him.

Over the next few months, Grant allowed God to enter into his heart and truly minister to him about His word. He was so delighted and found out that science is great, but it has its place. He found that God explains what scientists cannot about the creation of the world. Grant was excited because God allowed him to continue in science and fight for Him instead of against Him. He learned God's word and science goes hand in hand.

He hadn't thought about Stephanie. She came to mind once in a while, but he was focused on God. He left the loose women alone and even found him a set of new friends from his home church. Xavier is still his best friend, though. Grant is seeing clearer now and so much more than he's ever been. He finally understood what the big fuss was about and what Mr. Chase wanted him to see. He called Stephanie's father one afternoon and offered to take him to dinner. Mr. Chase gladly accepted. He liked the places Grant would take him because it was always fancy, and Mr. Chase hardly ever got to see that part of the world.

The fellas got together on a Friday night and went to one of those "down-home" laid back restaurants. Mr. Chase was kind of taken back by this being the fact he was looking forward to something elegant. They sat down and talked about everything and Grant's new-found faith in Jesus Christ. Mr. Chase was shocked, and he could tell Grant was sincere. He didn't even mention Stephanie as he talked with her father. All he talked about was what happened to him with God and explained why he didn't believe there was a God. Grant flowed so in the spirit that Mr. Chase was stunned and didn't know how to react. Then he asked Grant, "Why don't you come and revisit our church?"

"I appreciate that, but I have my own church that I love," Grant said because he still didn't agree with their pastor's teaching.

"I understand. Well, whenever you get a chance, you are welcome to come and visit," Mr. Chase added.

"Thank you."

Grant said his goodbyes to Mr. Chase and went about his way. They had a good conversation about God. Mr. Chase didn't let it be known unto Grant that he couldn't wait to go home and tell Stephanie what they talked about, but little did he know Miss Stephanie was out on her own date. She finally figured that it was time to move on. She'd mopped around long enough. Her best friend set her up on a date with a guy who went to her church. Stephanie was skeptical, but she did it anyway.

As she prepared for her date, she was nervous. Stephanie hadn't felt like that since Grant. She didn't know what to expect and did everything within her power to look good enough to eat. They were going to meet at the theatre to watch some 'ol sappy movie; is what Stephanie thought. She is an action movie junkie, but he doesn't know that.

Stephanie was supposed to be looking for a man wearing a pink button-down shirt, a silver sports jacket, and dark blue jeans. When she walked up in the place, she saw precisely that and thought to herself, "I am going to cut Arielya!" She rolled her eyes to the back of her head as he approached her and inquired, "Stephanie?"

"Gawd, yes," Stephanie grudgingly.

"I'm sorry, but is everything okay?" he asked.

"Yes," she answered.

"I'm Eric," he introduced.

"Nice to meet you, Eric," she responded kindly, trying not to lose her Christianity to call her friend Arielya and give her a few choice words. Though Eric could dress, smelled good, and apparently had himself together, he looked like somebody scrapped him along the concrete since birth.

"Are you ready to watch the movie?" he asked, pulling her out of a distant state.

"Actually, no," she answered.

"Why?" he asked.

"I'm not really a sappy, chick flick kind of girl. I like action movies," she answered.

"For real?" he shouted, sounding relieved.

"Yeah," Stephanie said.

"That's good to hear. I just assumed that you would like that movie."

"Nope, not me."

"I got the perfect movie. Do you mind if I choose?"

"No, go ahead. I want to see what kind of taste you have."

Eric turned to the attendant and said, "Two for Rock and a Hard Place." As he bought their tickets, a female approached Eric and said, "Is this what you do when I'm not around!"

"Girl, you need to go on with that foolishness! We ain't together no more," Eric responded.

"And who are you?" this mysterious woman asked.

"Sweetie, you got the wrong one. I don't owe you an explanation. Uhm, Eric, I'm going to go and pay for my popcorn and let you handle this," Stephanie said as she walked away.

"Stephanie, you don't have to go anywhere. I have nothing left to say to you, Shara. Let it go. We are over, and this is the main reason why," Eric said and tried to walk away, and that's when Shara made a scene.

"Don't think you are going to walk away from me! And you, don't you ever call me "sweetie" again! I will set it off up in here!" Shara yelled.

"Eric, this is too much for me. You need to get a handle on ya girl. I don't do drama…and this…this is drama," Stephanie said as she walked off, baffled about what just happened. She couldn't believe that this chick was going coo-coo over somebody that looked like when his momma gave birth to him, she boxed him in the face. Then on top of that, the chick Shara is gorgeous, "I don't get it…I know I'm a virgin, but homey must be working with something special," she thought to herself. Stephanie left Eric to deal with his "problems." On her way out, she called her friend and fussed her out about what happened.

"Oh, my bad. I thought that was over," Arielya said.

"My bad? What do you mean…my bad?" she asked.

"That chick is crazy about Eric, but I thought she was out of the picture," Arielya said.

"Why would you even set me up with somebody with those kinds of problems? You know me, and you knew I wouldn't deal with that," she said.

"Man, she used to come up in our church and set it off all the time. Our pastor had to sit down and talk with Eric about it too. That's why I thought it was a done deal because we didn't see her anymore after that," Arielya said.

"She may not be showing up in church, but she poppin' up at theatres," Stephanie rebutted.

"Girl, you are so crazy," Arielya said, laughing.

"I'm serious. You know I am not about all that drama, and Arielya, that was nothing but drama," Stephanie said.

"I'm sorry, Steph. I will talk to him about that," Arielya said.

"Oh, and another thing," Stephanie began to say.

"What! There's more?" Arielya asked, stunned.

"Yes, ma'am! How are you going to set me up with somebody that looks the way he looks?" Stephanie snapped.

"I know he may not be the most attractive…," she said.

"Most? Arielya, you've got to be kidding me. Homeboy is not pullin' his weight in the looks department," said Stephanie.

Arielya spit out the drink she was drinking because she busted out laughing. Then she calmed down and said, "But Stephanie, he is the sweetest person you will ever meet, plus he has a good head on his shoulder, and he is going places," she said.

"That's fine, and all, cause he gone need those other things going for him," she answered.

"What you pass up, someone else is willing to take," Arielya said.

"I don't mind. They can take him," Stephanie said with all seriousness.

"What about Grant? Are you willing for someone else to take him?" she asked.

"Don't go there, Arielya! Let that alone," she answered.

"I'm just saying Stephanie…," she said.

"Well, stop saying," she said.

"Alright," Arielya said reluctantly.

"I will talk to you later," Stephanie said.

"Okay, girl," Arielya said as they both hung up the phone.

The ladies got off the phone, and Arielya had Stephanie thinking about Grant. She doesn't know how long it took for her to stop thinking about him, and now Stephanie can't get Grant off her mind. She had a bad night all around. Stephanie headed home and got straight in the bed. She didn't say anything to her parents, and with the look on her face, they let her be. Mr. Chase didn't get a chance to tell her the good news. He knew Grant's change would ultimately amend her plans for marrying him.

Chapter Three: Rekindled Fire

It is coming up on Stephanie's birthday within a few hours, and she hardly wants to roll out of bed. She had her life all planned out, and it wasn't turning out how she wanted. As a little girl, Stephanie mapped out her life. She was going to graduate from college, work as a chef in a fancy restaurant, learn how to open her own business, at twenty-one get married, at twenty-three have her first baby, and so on; however, things didn't end up that way. Here it is, she's about to be twenty-four years old and only accomplished two of her many goals.

Meanwhile, four months have passed since Grant's transformation. She hasn't heard from Grant, nor has her dad told her about the change because he figured Grant would have called her by now, and the restaurant she's working at seems to be a dead end. Stephanie feels like she needs a change of scenery. She's given serious thoughts about moving away from home to another state and has already started the process by sending out her resume. She's receiving callbacks, but none of them feel right. She hasn't spoken to her parents about the move because she's not sure of the reaction she will get. The only thing she is sure of, and that is God, but even that seems a little shaky lately. Stephanie loves Grant, but she dares not turn her back on God because of love, and that's what is frustrating her most. She saw what it has done to her friends and family's relationships and the damage they cause themselves in the midst of it. She even feels like it's time to change churches. Stephanie grew up in the church she was in and loves it but feels like the time has come to break away.

As Stephanie is thinking about her life, she gets out of bed and walks to the kitchen to get something to eat, only to find that no one is home. She wondered why it was so quiet at 12:30 in the afternoon. It's never this hush, hush, either her mom is cooking in the kitchen or people running in and out of the house buying her mom's food, or her siblings clownin' in the living room. It's quiet as kept around there, which is cool because she doesn't want to talk to anyone anyway.

Loathing, Stephanie gets dressed, eats, and heads out to the mall. Arielya met her there, and they bought some outfits, got manicures and pedicures, laughed, and joked around. Stephanie was feeling pretty good. Her birthday was turning out to be alright. Mr. and Mrs. Chase called her and wished her a happy birthday and were begging her to come home so they could take her out to eat. She didn't want to disappoint her parent's dinner invitation, so she went back. When she arrived, they all prepared to go out for the evening. Her parents always took her out to eat for her birthday, and she enjoys it. Stephanie put on one of her new outfits and was feeling fly. She knew she looked good; even her dad said, "I'm going to have to take my gun with me tonight." It made her feel like the prettiest girl alive.

The family headed out to the restaurant Stephanie worked at, and she was not pleased. She was baffled as to why her parents would take her to the place she works on her day off. She tried not to trip though because she knows they wanted to take her someplace nice, but they don't have a lot of money. Stephanie got out of the car with a fake smile on her face. They walked in, and the waiter greeted them and acted as if he didn't know Stephanie. He took them to their table and left the menus with them. Mrs.

Chase left to go powder her nose. Stephanie and her father were enjoying each other's company. She almost forgot she worked there. It took her mother a long time in the restroom, so Stephanie went to check on her. Mrs. Chase was fine. It just took her a minute. They laughed about it and then walked back to the table to find Mr. Chase had left. They looked for him, but no one knew where he went. They walked around the restaurant to no avail. Stephanie led her mom to a back room, and when she opened the door, a loud noise yelled, "Surprise! Happy Birthday, Stephanie!" She could have died right there. Everyone was present. She said, "Y'all got me good!" One by one, they came up to hug her. When the last person walked up to her, he said, "Happy Birthday, Steph," and gave her the biggest hug of the night. He did not let her go for a long time. It was then she melted and really gave thought to leave her standards behind. Everyone was oohing and awing.

"I missed you, Steph," he said.

"I missed you too, Grant," she said as small tears slowly began to roll down her face.

"It was hard staying away from you, but I got what it was you were saying to me," he whispered in her ear.

"And what was that?" she asked.

"I want to thank you for leading me to Christ," Grant said, squeezing harder.

As she heard the sincerity in his voice, she cried softly. Everyone at that point dispersed to different sides of the room and held their own private conversations, leaving them alone to talk. They all knew the longing they had for one another and the struggles they went through, and for that reason, they ate and talked amongst themselves until the "love birds" finished their reunion.

"My offer still stands. It was never taken off the table. I would love to have you as my wife," Grant proposed.

"Really?" Stephanie said.

"I even have your father's blessing…both of them," he said.

"Both of them?"

"Your Father in heaven and your earthly father."

"Uhmmm…if I wasn't a virgin, you could have me right now."

Grant laughed and said, "I missed your sense of humor."

"Funny thing is, that wasn't a joke."

"I didn't have your Heavenly Father's permission the first time, and that is why I was turned down. I should have gone to Him first, and we wouldn't have had to go through all of this, but it did teach me something."

"And what was that?"

"It taught me I have to be careful about what I do as a husband because it could cause chaos in our lives if I don't do it right."

"Did I say yes, already?"

"No, you didn't."

"My answer is yes."

"Hold on, I want to do this in front of everybody."

Grant said, "Can I have everyone's attention, please?" Once they quieted down and looked his way, he got down on one knee and said, "From the first day I saw you, I never forgot you…that day at the expo. Then when I saw you in Florida, I knew I had to get with you. Steph, you are different than anyone I've ever known. You touch me in places only God would allow. It killed me inside when you said no to me the first time, but it eventually led me to life, and that's the kind of woman I want beside me for the rest of my days; a woman that's going to cause me to find life in all that I do. Stephanie Chase, will you marry me and become my help meet for the rest of my days?"

"Yes, Grant, yes," Stephanie answered as she cried.

Everyone cheered and clapped. Mr. and Mrs. Chase ran to hug their daughter, though they knew of Grant's plan all along. Mr. Chase held on to his daughter and said, "Happy Birthday, baby girl. Daddy loves you and wishes you the best in life."

"You know I am going to cater the food," Mrs. Chase said, crying and hugging her daughter.

"I love you, mom and dad," Stephanie cried.

This night was turning out better than she could have dreamed. Just when she thought about giving up her standards when Grant hugged her, she found she didn't have to. God was there from the beginning to make her life whole.

They all finished the night eating, laughing until the restaurant closed. The manager came to the room and wished his chef a happy birthday as well, and her gift was to have the next day off and with pay. Who could have asked for a better birthday?

Once everyone left, it was just Grant and Stephanie catching up on the time they missed out with one another. They went back to Grant's place, and before they knew it, they talked the whole night away in his living room on his couch. Stephanie realized it was six-thirty in the morning and said, "Awh man, it's time for me to go home."

"Can we have breakfast first?"

"Where do you want to go?"

"I don't know. We can pick up something small, and I will drop you off at home."

"That sounds good because I don't want to sit down anywhere to eat. I'm ready to go to sleep."

"Me too, but man, it felt so good sitting here and talking to you like we used to."

"I know."

They left the house and did as they planned to do. Grant walked her to the door and gave her a kiss goodbye. Stephanie came into the house, and it was still quiet. Apparently, mom and dad stayed out too, which was great because she didn't want to deal with what they thought happened or didn't happen because she stayed out all night with Grant.

Stephanie slept well into the afternoon. A wild dog picking a fight with a cat couldn't have awakened her. Grant was sleeping too. He slept with such peace, more peace than he's had in a long time. Later on, that evening, Grant came over to Stephanie's house and had dinner with the family. It was nice.

After dinner, Grant and Stephanie went to the movies. They went to see an action movie. Grant is always relieved that Stephanie isn't really into chick flicks. He feels like it's a second salvation. They loved the movie and were all smiles and talked about it on the way out of the theatre. Then someone said, "That was a good movie, wasn't it?"

"Yeah, man, it was," Grant said.

"How are you doing, Stephanie?" the man said.

"Oh, my bad, you know him, babe?" Grant asked, kind of caught off guard.

"Yes, this is Eric," she answered.

"How are you doing, Eric? I'm Grant, Stephanie's fiancé," he said.

"Nice to meet you, Grant. Stephanie, I didn't know you were engaged," Eric said.

"We got engaged last night," she said.

"Look, Stephanie, I never got to apologize about what happened that night," Eric said.

"Don't worry about it. Arielya explained your unique situation," Stephanie said.

"I still want to apologize, anyway. I'm sorry. Shara had no right to come at you like that," Eric said.

"It's cool. I hope things work out for you," she said.

"I know it will. You guys enjoy your night," Eric said, leaving.

"You too," Stephanie and Grant said simultaneously.

As they walked away, Grant asked Stephanie, "You went out with him?"

"It was short…real short. Arielya set me up with him trying to get me over you," Stephanie said.

"Man!"

"That was my reaction when I walked up to the movies to meet him. I was furious when I saw him."

"I was going to say…"

"Grant, please just don't say anything."

"You know I'm going to clown you, right?"

"Don't."

"Why are you acting like that? Was the date that bad?"

"I don't even want to talk about it."

Stephanie went on to explain her distaste for Eric. Grant laughed, which made her mad. She wasn't pleased with the situation at all. He continued to laugh, then dropped her off at home and prepared for work the next day.

After a few months down the road, everyone involved was working on the wedding; Stephanie and Grant took a break and hung out with each other. They were relaxing in his apartment. He was in the kitchen, cooking them something to eat. She was sitting on the floor, looking at some of his baby pictures.

"Awh…look at the cute wuttle baby," Stephanie said.

"What are you talking about?" Grant asked.

"I think we should put this naked baby in our video."

"Quit playing, Steph."

"I'm serious. Let me call my mom and tell her to add this picture to the video."

"I'm telling you, Steph; you better not do that."

She picked up her cell phone and began to "fake" dial home. Grant came out of the kitchen, running after her. Stephanie jumped up, and they ran around the coffee table, laughing.

"Don't like being laughed at, huh?" she asked.

"I'm going to get you!" Grant said.

He came across the table, and Stephanie yelled, "Ahhh!" Then she made a dash for the closest room, his bedroom. Grant stopped, smiled, and looked back as if he's acknowledging the readers of this book. He pimp-walked into the room after her and said, "Where are you going to go? You are in my domain now, and nobody knows it better than me."

"Oh, I can get out of here."

He backed her up against the wall and said, "Something tells me you don't want to get away, and neither does Ruby."

"Whatever, Grant."

She held the picture in her hand and stretched her arm upward like he couldn't reach it. Grant said, "Really, Steph?" She looked at him like, what? Then he shook his head and said, "Okay, since you want to play this game. I can make that picture hit the floor without even touching it." Stephanie replied, "Can you?" It was then he caressed her arm, and they stared into each other's eyes. Grant kissed his fiancé with such seduction that she melted and made up her mind to give in to this wonderful man and the temptation. They kissed up against the wall passionately. He was causing her to feel things in her body that reminded her about when she called him for the first time. "Ruby" was in full effect. She became weak and lost the will to hold onto the picture because she was caught up in the moment. Out the corner of his eye, he saw the photo fall to the floor. He stopped kissing her, stood back, and said, "I told you." Then he picked it up and started to walk off.

"What are you doing?" Stephanie asked.

"I got what I came for," Grant answered.

"Oh, so, you don't want this?"

"Oh, I want it, but not right now. Plus, what about Ruby, your jewel-friend?"

"Ruby is good with it. Oohh…Ruby is sooo good with it."

"Well, what good is a jewel that is accessible to everyone?"

"What good is a jewel if no one ever sees it?" Stephanie said as she walked up on Grant, pulling him closer to her by his oversized belt buckle.

As he kissed her, Stephanie began taking off his shirt. Grant asked, "Are you sure you are ready for this?"

Stephanie answered with a fiery kiss. He grabbed his soon-to-be wife and held on to her. Grant slipped off her shirt, and after that, she leaped and wrapped her legs around his waist. He carried her over to the bed and laid her down ever so gently. Then Grant stared into Stephanie's eyes and asked her one more time, "Baby, are you sure about this?" and she answered, "Yes, I am sure." Just the fact he kept asking made her want to give in even more. Stephanie hadn't been so sure about anything in her life. She is ready to give in to this pleasure. Grant explored her body with his hands softly, then as soon as he put his fingers on the button of her pants, the phone rang.

"Are you serious?" Grant said.

"You don't have to answer it," Stephanie said.

He checked his phone and said, "I have to. It's my mom."

"You can call her back," Stephanie said, pulling him closer to her.

"Let me answer the phone."

"A'ight."

"Hey, mama," Grant said, answering the phone call. "Why did it take you so long to answer your phone?" his mom asked. "Steph is over, and we were going over some pictures for the video. I'm cooking us something to eat," he answered. "Tell Stephanie I said hello," his mom said.

"Steph, mama said hello," Grant relayed the message.

"Hi, Ms. Bennet," Stephanie yelled from the background as she put back on her shirt.

"Grant, I called because I wanted to drop some things off to you, and I'm coming down your street now. Is it okay if I stop by?" his mom asked.

"Yes, mama. That is fine. Come on up. The door will be unlocked," Grant said.

"Alright, I'll be there in about five minutes, so put on some clothes," Ms. Bennet said.

"We are dressed, momma. See you when you get here," Grant said.

"Uh, huh, okay," Ms. Bennet said as she hung up the phone.

Grant put back on his shirt, went into the living room with Stephanie, and asked, "Are you okay?"

"Yes, but kind of disappointed."

"Don't be. We have the rest of our lives to make love."

"I know, but I am ready now."

"Steph, there is a reason that my mom called. She never just "stops by." God did that. Yes, you are my soon-to-be wife, but you are not my wife yet. You are worth more than Ruby. Her price is high, but you are a jewel yourself, and your price is higher than Ruby's. These are the situational decisions I was telling you about. I should have stopped it before the phone rang. I knew better. I want you just as bad as you want me, but we got to do this right. I don't want us to make another mistake."

Hearing those words upon her ears drew her closer to him. She straddled him on the floor, and said, "See, saying stuff like that makes me want to jump in the bed with you."

"Seriously, though, you are going to have to get off a brother. You are playing with fire and bothering my "ace." I'm trying to do right business here, and you are not making it easy."

"But, I'm ready, Grant."

"No, you are not Stephanie Chase. You will never forgive yourself if you go through with it, and I'm not going to allow you to do that to yourself."

"Hater," Stephanie said, laughing, getting off him.

"Believe. You will experience "ace" soon enough."

"I am going to make you crumble. You ain't nothing but a man, and all I have to do is pull out some tricks, so you will give in to my treats."

"That's where you are wrong. I run this, not you. Steph, you a little girl playing a grown man's game."

"But I know the game."

"Baby, you may think you know the game but not well enough to play it. Take a cold shower and calm down."

"You think you just said something don't you?"

"I know I did, and that's why you asked," Grant said, and they both smiled.

They sat on the floor, looking at pictures as she sat in between his legs laying back on him. A few moments later, Ms. Bennet walked in, and it brought a smile to her face to see her son happy with one woman. It quickly reminded her of how she and his father used to be and hoping that her son doesn't end up like them.

Ms. Bennet brought some things over for the wedding. She sat and talked with them for hours. It was needed because she missed her son. She would talk to him over the phone but would hardly come by. He reminded her of his father, and it was hard on her. Grant knew it too. He loved his mom, but it really bothered him that she couldn't look past who he looked like to see who he is. Stephanie left after a while, so they could talk. She wanted to get home to talk to her mom, as well.

Immediately as Stephanie walked through the door, she rushed to her mother. Mrs. Chase was watching television in her bedroom relaxing, and here comes her daughter to mess that all up.

"Momma, can I talk to you?" Stephanie asked.

"Now? I'm watching my shows," Mrs. Chase said.

"It's important, momma, please," Stephanie begged.

"Alright, but it better be good and juicy," Mrs. Chase said with a grin.

"You ain't right, momma," Stephanie said.

"What's on your mind, suga?"

"I almost had sex with Grant today."

Mrs. Chase pointed the remote at her daughter and said, "Thank you, Lifetime."

"Momma, I'm serious."

"I'm sorry, baby, but I had to lighten the blow."

"Momma, Grant makes me feel things in my body that I've never felt before. I was ready to give up my virginity, and still am."

"Well, he is a fine young man."

"Momma!"

"I'm just saying dumplin'. I may be old, but I ain't blind. What does Grant have to say about this?"

"He actually stopped it, but I wanted to keep going. He told me that I'm not his wife yet, and he wanted us to do things the right way."

"You don't want to hear this, but he is right, angel. I don't know how else to say it. I have to come to you with God's word. Yes, sex is pleasurable, and it feels good, but it feels even better when it's done in the right way. You do not see how you will feel after sex because you're blinded by the anticipation and the wiggly jiggly things going on in your body. Don't let the devil deceive you. Stephanie, sweetheart, you've waited this long; don't let go at the end. That's when you hold on the tightest."

"Thank you, momma."

"Anytime, sweetheart. I know it's rough, but you can make it through this."

"You always know what to say," Stephanie said as she hugged her mother and got up in the bed with her to watch television.

"Now that "Lifetime" is over, can we watch some TV?"

"You are so wrong for that momma."

The two ladies watched their favorite shows, laughing together. Stephanie loves her mother a lot. She does everything with her and desires to be like her in every way. She shares with her mother all that she goes through and asks her opinion on everything, but she will have to learn that she may not be the best option when she gets married. Mrs. Chase was relieved to hear that her daughter didn't have sex. Even though Stephanie is twenty-four years old, she is still considered "her baby." It would have broken her mother's heart had she went ahead and given away her virginity before time.

Chapter Four: Trouble in Paradise

Earlier within that year when Stephanie was considering that big move and working on things to make it happen, one of the jobs came through that she sent a resume to. Still, the only issue is, she forgot to tell Grant about her plans. She gave it no more thought after Grant proposed to her; therefore, this job interview that she has in Jacksonville, FL, in a week has thrown her for a loop. Her wedding is vastly approaching in a few weeks, and she believes this will put a damper on their plans. Stephanie has no idea how Grant will take the news, especially since he hasn't had time to put in applications himself.

They have a date tonight, and this is not a way to start off the weekend. Stephanie got dressed in some clothes that this news may slide by Grant a little easier. She is even going to pay for the meal. "How am I going to break the news to him?" is what she always thought. It ran through her mind a thousand times. She rehearsed what she would say and how she would say it…maybe at the restaurant, so there won't be a scene. She only has an hour left before Grant picks her up.

Mrs. Chase recognized that her daughter had something on her mind. She isn't sure what it is, but she can tell that it's serious. Mrs. Chase always taught her daughter to talk to someone if something is bothering her to the point of distress; maybe they can shed some light on the situation. Hesitantly Mrs. Chase says, "Stephanie, baby, what's wrong?"

"Nothing, momma," Stephanie replied.

"Something is on your mind, and it's heavy. I can see it. Maybe if you talk about it, you will feel better."

Being the fact she hadn't even let her mother in on her plans, she didn't want to talk to her about it either because she knows it would hurt her mother. "Momma, really, I don't want to talk about it."

"I promise you will feel better if you do."

She paused and sighed, then said, "Sit down, momma. There is something that I have to tell you."

"You're not pregnant, are you?"

"No, momma. I'm good on that end."

"Well, what is it dumplin'?"

"Momma, while Grant and I were apart, it was hard for me."

"I know it was baby."

"So, I made some decisions about my life. I put in applications in other states and sent out resumes…"

"I do not like where this is going."

"After we got back together, I forgot about everything and let it go. But obviously, the resumes were still working because I received a call a few days ago about a job offer. I'm going down to Jacksonville, FL this week for an interview, and the biggest problem I have is that Grant doesn't know about it."

"Why didn't you tell me, Steph? Me, of all people…I thought we were closer than that. I can't believe you didn't tell me that you wanted to leave," her mom said, running to her bedroom and closing the door.

"I knew I shouldn't have told her," Stephanie mumbled to herself.

Mrs. Chase was crushed. She loves her daughter and quiet as kept she always favored Stephanie. They did everything together. It is one thing for her daughter to get married, but it's a whole other ball of wax to move to another state. Mrs. Chase didn't know if she could take that. She wouldn't get to see her daughter every day like she does now…not even every week. If her mother reacted like that, she could only imagine what Grant is going to say.

Moments later, Grant came to the door to get Stephanie. She yelled to her mother she was going out and she will be back, but Mrs. Chase didn't answer at all. She walked out of the house with her head down. Grant knew something was wrong because it wasn't like Mrs. Chase not to answer Stephanie. She would always see her daughter out when Grant came to get her. This reaction caused Grant to start with the twenty questions, but Stephanie avoided them. They went out to eat, but she hardly ate a bite of food. He couldn't take the silence anymore, so he paid for the food and took Stephanie to a quiet place to talk.

Once they arrived at his place, Grant said, "Okay, Steph, what is going on?"

"I don't know how to tell you, Grant," Stephanie said reluctantly.

"Your best bet is to just say it, Stephanie. You've been quiet all evening, nor did you tell me what happened that upset your mom so badly."

"Okay…well…here it is. While we were broken-up, I made some decisions about my life. The break-up was hard for me. I couldn't stay around here with a chance of running into you. I wanted a change and missed you so much. After thinking things over, I sent out my resume…"

"Okay, what's wrong with that?"

"I sent them to other states."

Grant paused and gave a blank stare. Stephanie finished saying, "Then once we got back together, I forgot all about it and let it go with no more thought and…"

"And?"

"I received a call last week to come in for a job interview in Jacksonville."

Grant sat back on the couch and didn't say anything. Stephanie didn't know what to say. She was scared to whisper a word. She stood up and started to walk towards the door. Then Grant finally spoke, saying, "Get back here and sit down. You are going to finish this."

Stephanie walked back to the couch and did as Grant insisted and said, "What do you want me to say?"

"I want you to say that there is nothing to say…nothing to talk about because it's not even an option. That's what I want you to say."

"Grant, this could be good for us."

"For us? No, for you. What am I supposed to do, Stephanie?"

"But this was before we got back together."

"And you didn't feel the need to tell me after we got back together."

"I promise, I totally forgot with the wedding plans and all."

"That's no excuse Steph."

"I know, and I'm sorry, Grant."

"Where do we go from here?"

"I don't know. You tell me."

"I don't want to move. I love it here."

"Will you go to the interview with me; then once we see where it is and check out the location and what it has to offer, we make a decision then?"

"I don't want to, but for you, I will. Stephanie, this can't happen again. You have got to communicate with me. I'm not liking this at all."

"Thank you, Grant, and again, I'm sorry," Stephanie said as she scooted closer to him and gave him a kiss on the check.

"Don't do that," Grant said as he backed away from her.

"Do what?" Stephanie said as she was kissing him on his neck.

"That…stop playing. Now is not the time, and honestly, I can't say that I would stop you this time. You have pissed me off, and now you're doing this out of guilt."

"Ugh!" Stephanie whined.

"I'm taking you home. I need a minute."

"I don't know who I hurt worse, you or momma. I'm ready to go but take me over Arielya's instead."

"Alright."

It was a quiet ride. Stephanie wanted to say something but wasn't sure if she would make it worse. Grant didn't say a word, nor did he feel as if he should say anything. He dropped her off at Arielya's without so much as an "I love you." He was in disbelief she would pull this, and it wasn't so much the job offer as it was that she NEVER said anything about it. She had plenty of chances to mention the decision she made concerning her life. He didn't mind moving, but he felt like she could have at least given him time to react. There is no time to react, and they are going to be married in a few weeks.

Once Arielya answered the door, Stephanie broke down in tears. "What's wrong, Stephanie?" Arielya asked as she put her arms around her and led her to the couch.

"I messed up," Stephanie answered.

"What did you do?" Arielya asked.

"Remember when Grant and I were broken up?" she asked.

"God, yes," Arielya answered.

"Anyway, I wanted to make some changes in my life. I wasn't sure if our situation would change. I didn't hear from him for a while…he quit chasing, and I wasn't budging, so I figured why stay around here. Well, I put in some applications at other restaurants in other states, and whoever bit first, that's who I was going to go with."

"Stephanie, you are trying to move? Why didn't you tell me?"

"When Grant and I got back together, I forgot all about it."

"So…"

"So, what?"

"So…if you forgot about it, why is it still a big deal?"

"Because I was called last week for a job interview…in Jacksonville, FL."

"Congratulations!"

"Not so, Grant is ticked at me. When he dropped me off, he didn't say a word to me."

"So, what are you going to do, Steph?"

"I don't know. I really want to take hold of this job opportunity, but Grant, on the other hand, is furious. I don't want to stay here anymore, Arielya. I grew up in Savannah, and it's time to go. I feel as though I've done all that

I can do here. And now, for me to continue to grow, I need to cut away from Savannah."

"I hear you, but why didn't you let Grant know. You got to see it from his point. After you guys got engaged, that may have been a good time for you to share this with him. I would be mad with you too!"

"Don't say that, Arielya. My mom is mad at me too."

"You didn't even tell Mama Chase! Ah, yeah, you done bumped your head. Do you know what you mean to your mother? That's cold, Stephanie…real cold."

"I didn't feel the need to say anything because I wasn't sure if anyone would give me a chance since I'm new in the chef business. I wasn't trying to be cold, Arielya…just cautious."

"Well, that blew up in your face, didn't it?"

"Yeap, and I don't know what to do."

"First thing you must do is give Grant his room. It's a lot to process. He's going to come around. Meanwhile, prepare yourself for this job interview."

"But what about…"

"Oh, no, miss, missy, you are going. You might as well pack it up along with your mouth and set sail for Jacksonville, FL, or you will regret it for the rest of your life."

"I know. I didn't want to hurt anybody Arielya."

"I know, but you have to give them time to make sense of it all. They have to realize you deserve to be happy too. We don't know why God does what He does, but there is a reason for everything He allows."

"You right."

"I know I am."

"Girl, you are so crazy."

"I try."

"Can I sleep on the couch?"

"Girl, please, sleep in the other bedroom."

"Thanks, Arielya…for everything."

"You're welcome, boo."

Stephanie went to sleep but didn't get any real rest. She tossed and turned…no call from Grant, not even a text. At this point, his love was just as silent as his nonverbal words. Her mother hadn't called either. Arielya was the only one who understood Stephanie and why she must do this.

Sometimes in life, opportunities are thrown at us, and it's up to us whether we seize the moment or whether we allow for the opportunity to wither away like a flower. Do we allow circumstances around us to keep us from taking hold of the break that we've been praying for? If this open door is for us, then all things will work out, but if not, then nothing will work out. This is why it's important to seek the Lord in whatever decisions we make or plans that we have. We will know in our hearts whether the opportunity is from God or not. If we decide without Him, then we can't very well expect for everything to fall in place and for all things to work out. We must depend on Him for all our decisions.

The next morning Stephanie woke up and fixed her and Arielya some breakfast. Many things are still running through her head from last night, but she ultimately decided to follow the comfort she received from the Holy Spirit. She made up her mind to go to the interview and give it all she's got. Stephanie is determined to get this job no matter what anybody says. She hopes Grant calls, but it's not going to ruin her day.

Once Stephanie finished cooking breakfast, she put it on a tray and took it to her best friend to thank her for her love and encouragement. She had breakfast looking nice and very elegant.

"Good morning Arielya."

"Girl, what is this?"

"Just my little way of saying thank you."

"You didn't have to do that."

"Oh, I know, but I did anyway."

"It is too early for you to be getting smart."

"I ain't worried about that. I still owe you one for setting me up on that date."

Realizing what her best friend just said about that date, it made her ask, "Is there something in my food?"

"No, I'm not going to mess up a nice concoction for that. I have other ways to get you."

"I knew I should have slept with one eye open and one eye closed last night."

They both laughed and ate breakfast together. Arielya didn't leave any food behind. She sopped it up. Stephanie got her things together to go home. About an hour later, she received a text from Grant saying he was coming to pick her up. She was thinking to herself she wished she would have driven her own car last night. "A rule of thumb; never get into an argument with your significant other when you decided not to drive that day," was

Stephanie's thought, although she was feeling a little uneasy about seeing him.

Arielya left for work before Grant could get there to pick up Stephanie. It was a few hours before she had to be at work herself. Finally, Grant came. He honked his horn for her to come out. She couldn't believe it…Grant honking his horn? She figured he must have gone crazy. She couldn't say much because she needed to get home and get ready for work.

"Thank you for picking me up. I didn't think you were coming," Stephanie said, getting into his car.

"I don't care how mad I am at you. I'm not going to leave you hanging," Grant said.

"That's good to know," Stephanie said.

"How was the rest of your night?" Grant asked.

"How do you think? I went to bed without my fiancé saying a word to me," she answered.

"If that's not the pot calling the kettle black. Now, you know how I feel. My fiancé didn't let me know of her plans, so I could change mine, or at least we could have compromised."

"I said I was sorry, Grant."

"I know you did, but that doesn't excuse what you did, Stephanie."

"Ok, so now you know. I messed up. I'm sorry. Where do we go from here?"

"We work it out, that's what."

Stephanie was glad to hear that, and it brought a smile to her face. She wasn't quite sure what would happen between them because Grant was pretty mad at her. She could care less what else comes after this because all she cared about was that he wouldn't break off the engagement. She asked him, "How do we do that?"

"A few things were on my mind last night. I was up all night thinking about it. The only thing I could come up with is, first, let's see if you get the job, and if you do, I will help you move down there."

"Are you not moving with me?"

"Let me finish."

"Go ahead."

"Once you get settled, I will look for work down there or get transferred, then I will move down there. We may be apart for a short time, but it's the best we can do right now."

"How long?"

"What do you mean?"

"How long will we be apart? Three months? Six months? Nine months?"

"However long it takes for me to get a job. I'm not moving there without a job or transfer, Stephanie. I am not nor have ever been a man depending on my woman to take care of me. It ain't gone happen."

"But Grant…"

"But nothing. That's it. I've made up my mind. You put me in this predicament, and I'm dealing with it the best way I can with what has been dealt to me."

"But don't I have a say in this?" Grant looks at her with a "are you serious" look, and she said, "Never mind."

"I'm not trying to be anal about it but make no mistake; I'm still pissed."

"That's fine. Just drop me off at home so I can get ready for work."

"Don't get an attitude. I didn't start this."

"You know what, that's it! I'm sick and tired of hearing that I was the one that caused this. I know I was, and I don't need you to keep reminding me of it. I said I was sorry. Now either you are going to forgive me and let it go or let me go. Take your pick."

"Oh, so you doing it like that now. I could have dropped you, but I didn't. I stay because I love you."

"Then if you love me, forgive me."

"I do love you, Steph, and you know I do, but the forgiving thing is going to take time. I'm just sayin' dawg give me some time. It ain't even been 24 hours."

"I'm not trying to break your heart, Grant. I'm really not."

"I know, but…"

"But, you got to know I love you. When we broke up, it was really hard on me."

"Me too."

"I needed a change. I didn't want to be here anymore. The restaurant I work at is awful, and there's no room for growth. Church wasn't the same, so I needed to find someplace else to go. All I knew is that I could no longer live here. I couldn't take the chance of running into you and didn't know how much more I could take of not being with you. I don't know a whole lot about relationships. You are the only one I've ever had a real relationship with, and this is all new to me. On the other hand, you have had many relationships, and I know while we were broken up, you had stuff going with other women. So look, I'm going to make mistakes, and it just so happens that I've made two big ones so far."

"That's an understatement," Grant said as they both looked at each other and broke out into a laugh. It was an intense moment on the ride home. Grant heard what his love was saying and decided to let it go. Then he continued saying, "You're right. I'm going to let it go, and if I'm going to support you, then I'm going to support you without bringing it back up."

"Thank you," Stephanie said as she leaned over and kissed Grant on his cheek.

"Don't forget our appointment tonight."

"What appointment?"

"What? Steph, seriously?"

"I'm just playin'. I will be at the church by seven o'clock."

"Don't play like that," Grant said as they pulled up to her place.

They said their good-byes and went on about their day. Before Stephanie put her key in the door, she paused and took a breather for the other battle she has to fight with her mom. After standing at the door for a few minutes, she finally went inside the house. When she walked past the living room, she didn't see or hear anybody. The only thing Stephanie heard was the television on in her mother's room in which the door was closed. She could tell her mom still didn't want to talk, so she headed straight for her room instead, and when she got there, her father was stretched out on her bed, looking towards the television that wasn't on.

"Daddy, what are you doing?" Stephanie asked.

"You know, when you were a little girl, I gladly watched you walk in your mother's footstep, and I said to myself, "She is going to make someone a beautiful wife someday…just like her mom." Now, I realize that time is upon us. My little girl is all grown up and leaving the nest."

"Daddy."

"I never thought, in my wildest dreams, that my little girl would leave Savannah. I just knew she would always be around."

"Daddy…" Stephanie said as her father cut her off and still hasn't looked her in the face. He's sitting up in her bed with the pillow propped up against the headboard, fully clothed with shoes and all, his legs crossed, and hands folded in his lap, on her frou-frou country red and white flowery bedspread. Mr. Chase continued saying, "I also thought if my baby girl needed anything or felt like she couldn't make it, that she would at least talk to her favorite person in the world about it, her mom."

"Daddy, you don't understand."

"I've never seen your mother so heartbroken, not even when your brother moved out."

"I never meant to hurt momma. When Grant and I got back together, I left all of that alone. I didn't know that a job would come open."

"Some blessings come when you least expect it when you're not looking for it and or when you're not focused on it."

"Blessings? Daddy, what are you saying?"

"I'm proud of my baby girl. I hope Grant understands, and soon your mom will too."

"I am proud of my favorite girl, too," Mrs. Chase said as she walked in, listening to her husband speaking to their daughter.

Stephanie turned around and gave her mom the biggest hug and said, "Momma, I'm so sorry. I never meant to hurt you."

Mr. Chase joined in the hug and left the room for them to talk. Mrs. Chase walked her daughter to her bed and sat her on the same frou-frou country red and white flowery bedspread and said, "Your father is right. It is a blessing. He talked to me last night and told me how selfish I was being."

"Daddy and his words," Stephanie said.

"Oh, honey, he set your momma straight," Mrs. Chase said, and Stephanie giggled. She finished by saying, "After I thought about what your dad said to me, I came to realize he was right. It was selfish of me wanting you to be here all the time. Stephanie, you have been at my hip ever since you were little, and I grew accustomed to that. If it was up to me, you would be here forever."

"No. she can't!" Mr. Chase yelled from the other room. The ladies laughed.

"Be quiet in there!" Mrs. Chase yelled back.

"Daddy is so crazy."

"Only for you puddin'. Only for you," Mr. Chase said.

"I hope Grant came to understand," Mrs. Chase said.

"He was livid, momma. We had it out. He dropped me off at Arielya's last night without so much as an I love you. Then this morning he came, picked me up, and we talked about everything."

"Are y'all good?"

"Yes, we're good."

Chapter Five: The Next Chapter Begins

The wedding is upon Grant and Stephanie. After the trip to Jacksonville, FL, she can add "Head Chef" to her resume. Grant was happy for her, although he'd rather stay in Savannah. However, he found out that the University of Jacksonville, FL, was there, and he could go back to school to get his master's degree. He graduated with his bachelor's degree about a year ago. His goal is a Ph.D.

Nevertheless, he tried hard to let go moving away, but he couldn't lie to himself. He hid how he felt for Stephanie's sake. They found a nice two bedroom apartment. They already moved Stephanie's things in it and bought new furniture. She arranged it with her new job at "Le Floures," a fresh new spot in town, to start a month after their wedding. Grant and Stephanie planned for their weekends and days off. They were only about two and a half hours away from Savannah. He would come down and be with her on the weekends, and she would go be with him on her days off.

Everyone is going crazy today. Getting people ready for the wedding was a rush. It starts at two o'clock. Stephanie was getting cold feet and felt like she really needed to see Grant before the wedding to make sure they were doing the right thing. She couldn't put her finger on it, but things weren't the same between them since the big argument. She called him on the phone, and they secretly found a place to meet.

"Is everything alright, sweetheart?" Grant asked.

"Yes and no," Stephanie said.

"What's wrong?" Grant asked, a little puzzled. He can't wait to marry the woman that changed his outlook on a lot of things.

"Grant, are we doing the right thing?" Stephanie asked.

"What do you mean, Stephanie?"

"Things seem to be different between us. I can't put my finger on it, but things haven't been the same, and I don't want either one of us to lie to ourselves or do something we don't want to do."

"Stephanie, I don't know about you, but I'm marrying the woman who changed my perspective about everything, especially God. I love you, Stephanie, and I'm not looking back."

"Well, what has been this thing between us? I know you feel it too."

"The only thing that's been bothering me…man…I didn't want to tell you."

"What is it, Grant?"

"I'm not ready to leave Savannah. It's hard to move."

"What's your attachment to Savannah? If anything, I thought you would want to get away from here."

"You should understand more than anyone. This is home to me."

"I do understand, but I also understand we need to start our own lives, together, a new journey in a new place. I love my family and want to stay, but I want what God has for me more."

"I guess that's true, but I'm only being honest with you, Steph."

"I know…so…where do we go from here?"

"We get married. I said I would miss Savannah, but I didn't say that I would choose it over you, Steph. I want you more than staying here. I know one thing, though."

"What do you know?" Stephanie asked as she stepped closer to him with her hands on his chest.

"I'm going to miss you."

"I'm going to miss you too."

"I don't want us to be apart, but it won't be long, hopefully."

"That's the one major thing I hate about all of this."

"Me too, but we will be together soon enough."

"Grant…"

"Yes, love."

"I'm glad I'm marrying you today. I've wanted this for so long."

Grant smiled as she stroked his ego and said, "I'd like to marry you now."

"Me too, but I know everybody is wondering where we are at."

"Alright then, I'll see you at the altar."

They kissed each other good-bye and went their separate ways to get themselves ready. As soon as Stephanie walked into the church, everyone rushed at her and questioning her concerning her whereabouts. She calmed them down and went to get ready for the wedding.

Arielya is Stephanie's maid of honor, and is making sure everything is going according to plan. Grant's oldest brother, Gianni, is his best man. Instead of the best man supporting the groom, he has continuously tried to talk him out of getting married even though he's married himself. Grant became irritated with his brother's constant lack of support and almost replaced him as best man with his best friend, Xavier, or his other brother Gavin. Gianni's wife, Clara, was doing the same thing to Stephanie, but she didn't have to put up with it because she did not include Clara in the wedding party.

As the guests arrived, by invitation only, a commotion in the foyer began to arise, and Arielya went to handle it. Upon her arrival in the foyer, she gazed upon a woman she didn't know and was the cause of the commotion.

"What's the problem?" Arielya asked the usher.

"This woman is trying to come in but doesn't have an invitation," the usher said.

"Ma'am, I'm sorry, but this wedding is by invitation only," Arielya said.

"I don't know who you are, but you and nobody else will stop me from seeing my lil cousin get married," the woman said.

"May I ask you your name?" Arielya said, trying to hold her peace and act professionally.

"Sherry," she answered.

"Ok, Sherry, it's nice to meet you. Let me check this out, and I will come right back to you. Would you please have a seat right here, and I will back?" Arielya said.

"Thank you," Sherry said.

Arielya went to Stephanie and asked her if she knew this woman. Just like Arielya thought, Stephanie didn't know this woman and never heard Grant talk about her either. Stephanie told her to just let the lady come in because she didn't want any further disruptions. Arielya said okay but went to talk with Grant about this so-called "cousin."

She walked to the other side of the church, and the more she walked, the angrier she became because this was taking away from her best friend's day. She knocked on the dressing room door like a madwoman and said, "I need to speak with Grant."

"What is it, Arielya? We are getting ready to start in a minute," Grant said as he stepped out the door.

"We've got a problem," Arielya said.

"What?" Grant responded.

"There is a woman who says she's your cousin and causing commotion because we won't let her in," she said.

"Why won't you let her in?" he asked.

"Because it's by invitation only, and quite frankly, I don't believe she's your "cousin,"" Arielya said.

"What's her name?" Grant asked.

"She says her name is Sherry."

"Sherry? I don't know of any cousin of mine whose name is Sherry."

"Stephanie said for me to just let the lady in, but I don't want to. What would you like for me to do?"

"Do as the bride requested but let me see who this woman is."

"All I'm going to say is this, you, betta put a handle on it, or I will, and this betta not be your chick on the side."

"You don't have to worry about that. I'm straight on my end and don't have anything to worry about."

Arielya went on about her way to get her best friend ready for what was going to take place in just a few minutes. Grant, however, never went to check on the lady. He figured since he didn't have anything to hide, he wasn't going to worry about it, plus he was focused on marrying Stephanie.

The musician started playing the organ, and the church was packed with guests. Grant, the best man, and groomsmen looked debonaire in their black tux with teal bowties and cummerbunds. The bridesmaids, maid of honor, and matron of honor were walking down the aisle looking beautiful in their teal gowns draped in silver coined sequence and teal open-toed shoes to match and the bouquets. Their hairstyles were all the same, pinned up and a few spiral curls falling from the pin-up. They were adorned with silver bracelets, a gift from Stephanie, with matching earrings.

Everyone stood up as the "Here Comes the Bride" song began to play. The doors opened, and everyone gasped at how beautiful she looked. Stephanie walked down the aisle with a smile on her face, wearing a white dress. She looked like someone out of a royalty magazine. Her dress was fitting and flared out beautifully at the end with a soft color of teal down the train's back. Her hair was pulled up in a French bun with spiral curls, and the veil covered her face.

Mr. Chase gladly walked his daughter to the altar then handed her to Grant, then went to his seat. He smiled at her, then took her by the hand. Both of their hands were trembling. The ceremony went on as planned. They both placed the rings they bought for each other on their fingers. Once they said their vows, Stephanie's childhood pastor said, "I now pronounce you husband and wife. You may kiss the bride." Grant pulled back the veil, fixed his eyes upon his wife with a small oval diamond piece on her forehead, and kissed his wife. Everyone stood up and clapped their hands.

Grant whispered in Stephanie's ear, giggling, "Get this reception over with so I give you what you've been waiting for." She laughed at him and said, "Just take me down the aisle."

As they walked up the aisle, exiting the sanctuary, he recognized the woman who said she was his cousin. Immediately he said to his new wife, "Stephanie, you see that woman right there?"

"Yes. Is that the one Arielya was talking about?"

"Uh, huh."

"What about her?"

"She is my ex-girlfriend from college."

"I thought she looked familiar. That's the one from the expo when we first saw each other."

"Yes, that's her."

"Well, what is she doing here?"

"I don't know, but I'm not going to let her spoil our day. I just wanted you to be forewarned in case she tried anything."

"Oh, Arielya got that. I'm not worried."

They went on to the reception, and "Sherry" went home. She wanted to see for herself if Grant was really over her, would he go through with this charade of marrying someone that was not "his type." When she saw that he did marry Stephanie, she decided to go home and let Grant go for good.

The reception was delightful and long. Grant was getting a little antsy and ready for the honeymoon. He kept playing with her legs up under the table, and when he tried to go up under her dress, she jumped up and yelled, "It's time for the toast!" Grant started laughing, and she couldn't keep from smiling. Nobody knew what was going on and why in the world was the bride jumping up talking about a toast when that is the best man's job. Eventually, Gianni said the toast, and it went a little something like this, "Grant, you are my little brother, and I love you, man. I wish this drink was whiskey instead of some sparkling juice. I don't want to sparkle. I want to drink." Everyone started laughing, then he continued, "No, but seriously, you have a beautiful wife. I believe she will make you happy. Always remember, though, money isn't going to make you happy, and it will run out, but love never will and will make your marriage last. Marriage is work, but you can endure it. Marriage will bring you joy. It will also bring troubles, and that is when you must stick together even the more." Grant's parents stared at each other across the room as they listened to their son give the toast, and these words were stricken upon their hearts. Gianni continued, "Work hard to not let the flame die out. I know this doesn't seem like a toast, but it is wisdom, and that is what I want to give to both of you tonight. It's the best gift you will ever receive in marriage. I love you both and wish you the best of happiness."

Everyone lifted their glasses and took a drink. Grant stood up and gave his brother a hug. He knew there was more behind his toast than he was letting on, but Grant decided to save that conversation for another day. The reception was over, and the guests sent Mr. and Mrs. Bennet off. They entered a white limousine, and the driver drove them to the airport. Grant was all over Stephanie, and she fought him off, laughing. They were smiling and kissing each other, talking, and enjoying the moment.

Grant planned for them to go to Jamaica for their honeymoon. They caught their flight and were off. He wished he could have given Stephanie first-class seats on the plane, but he just couldn't afford it. She could have cared less. She wasn't used to first-class anyway.

Grant is the "give my wife the world" type of person, and when he can't do that, he doesn't feel good about himself. He was used to the lifestyle of "first-class" because that's how he was raised. It was all about money. He is going to learn a lot during this marriage journey.

On the plane, they sat next to a businessman. He was sickened by the way Grant and Stephanie carried on, so much so, he voiced his opinion, "Could you two please tone it down? I'm trying to conduct business."

"Sorry man, we just got married," Grant said with googly-eyes. The man didn't respond. He went back to working on his computer. Then Grant said to him, "You know what it's like, man. I see that wedding ring on your finger."

"Look, young man, don't assume happiness just because you see a ring. I don't mean to put a damper on your parade, but sometimes things don't turn out how you thought they would," the businessman said.

"I don't know what you are going through, but God can make all things new. He can make things better. At the end of the day, it's a choice. You can choose to have a great marriage or even a great life, or you can let circumstances choose for you," Grant said.

"Well said, baby," Stephanie said.

"Thank you, Steph," Grant said.

"Y'all are young and don't know what you are talking about, and as far as God, I haven't seen Him do anything in my life. I hope you do not ever experience how I'm feeling right now. Still, the reality is, one day, you will," the businessman said and cut the conversation short.

Grant and Stephanie went on and enjoyed each other, forsaking the sour words of the bitter but obviously hurt businessman. He eventually moved to another open seat because he couldn't take it anymore.

When the plane landed, and everyone was leaving, the happy couple ran across the businessman. He said to them, "Hey guys, I'm sorry. I never should have said those things to you. It's hard to look at couples in a place where you used to be. I hope for the best for you guys."

"It's alright, and thank you. I hope things turn around for you and your wife," Grant said.

"Thank you, but I don't know what it will do because I'm on my way to meet my lawyer. We are dissolving our marriage today," the businessman said.

"What is your name?" Grant asked.

"Ted," he answered.

"Ted, I'm Grant, and we are going to pray for you," he said.

"Thank you," Ted replied.

"Whatever the outcome, don't give up on God. He hasn't given up on you, even though it doesn't feel like it," Grant said.

"That's an understatement," Ted said. All three of them sort of chuckled.

"God will make you smile again," Grant said.

"He did once, and I hope so again," Ted said.

"He will," Stephanie said.

"Well, I have to be going," Ted said.

"Alright, you take care," Grant said.

Grant and Stephanie went on about their way, said a prayer for Ted, checked into their hotel, and settled in their room. Stephanie was in awe of the white sand beach and the beautiful bluish-green water. She'd never seen anything like it, except on television. Then her hotel room made her jaw drop.

"Grant, this is nice," Stephanie said.

"I thought I would take you someplace you'd never been before," he said.

"The room is so big and has all of the amenities," Stephanie said.

"Check out my baby using big words."

"Shut up, Grant."

"I'm just sayin' baby. Don't get mad."

"Whatever."

"Now, I've waited long enough, and it's time for you to give it up."

"What!"

"Awh, don't act surprised. You know what time it is."

"Man, I ain't given you nothing. You ain't acting right."

"I see. I'm going to have to chase you around the room. You like me chasing you."

"Why do you say that?"

"Let's just say the last time I chased you, you were ready to give it up."

"Stop living in the past. That was then, and this is now. I've become a pro at the game."

"And still haven't mastered it."

"You think so, huh."

"Oh, I know so. The only way to master this game is going all the way, and I'm ready to help you become a master."

"Is that right?"

He walked up on Stephanie and said, "sho' you right," and passionately began kissing her. She kissed him back for a short second, then stepped away. Grant asked, "What's wrong? Is my breathe tart?" checking his breath.

Stephanie busted out laughing and said, "You're fine. I'm just not ready yet."

"Hold up, sistah, you are going to give it up. I got papers!"

"Well, while you are waiting for me to decide when I'm going to give it up, I'll be on the beach. See ya!" Stephanie said and started walking towards the door with a twist in her hips in her rainbow two-piece swimsuit and a tropical colored wrap.

"Okay, I see what's going on but remember this, you have to come back, and if you want to spend some money, and you will need money. By the way, would you like your purse back?"

"Uh…how…how did you get my purse? Man!"

"I know my wife, and she likes the chase."

"Well, I don't need my purse, nor do I want anything," Stephanie said as she took off her wrap while placing her right leg in a chair to put on her sandals.

"You will when your throat gets parched," Grant said, clearing his throat, watching as his wife was bending over.

"You ain't right. Come on, let's go to the beach Grant," Stephanie said as she bent all the way over, pretending to fix the bottom part of her sandals.

"Let's go tomorrow. We've had a long day, and honestly, all jokes aside, I'm spent," he said as he sneaked upon his wife.

"What do you think you're doing?" Stephanie said as she quickly stood up because she could feel him moving closer to her.

"I wanted to give you back your purse."

"I told you I don't need it."

"Get back here."

"Beach time!" Stephanie said with a smile.

Grant quickly ran up to his wife and snatched her up in his arms. Stephanie smiled with excitement. She broke loose and ran across the bed to try to get to the bathroom but failed miserably. Grant leaped and caught her by the ankles on the bed and said, "I got you now. You ain't going anywhere." Stephanie found it useless to keep running. For one, she was just as exhausted as he was, and two wanted him just as badly. Grant delved into four-play, discovering all the spots Stephanie allowed. The newlyweds were in the middle of the bed, consummating their marriage. Stephanie wasn't sure how it was supposed to feel. All she noticed is that it was more painful than pleasurable. Grant did his best in making sure he took his time with his wife, but he could tell it wasn't bliss for Stephanie.

Afterward, they didn't converse about it and headed out to eat; it was an awkward dinner. It's a shame. The view was beautiful, but the presence of discomfort was more of the scenery; words barely said, eye contact is scarce, and the restroom breaks were overdone.

"How long are we going to do this, Steph?"

"Do what?"

"You know…this."

"What's this?"

"Okay, Steph, are we going to play games or solve this problem?"

"I don't know what to say, Grant. What do you want me to say?"

"Something."

"I can't even form the words."

"I'll just go ahead and say it; the sex was weird."

"Yes, it was."

"How was it for you?"

"It was painful and dissatisfying."

"For real? That bad?"

"I don't mean it like that, Grant. I don't know how it's supposed to feel, but good wasn't one of them."

"It will get better, Steph. I tried my best to make it as comfortable as possible."

"I know you did, but like you said, it will get better as we keep practicing."

"Awh yeah, cause practice will be in full effect?"

"You can stop smiling. I want to, but not tonight. I am really sore."

"We'll get over this hump, but for now, let's enjoy this meal and head to the beach."

Grant and Stephanie were at ease now they've talked about the "elephant in the room," but Grant was confident he would change his wife's views about sex. Although, he did feel some type of way. He didn't expect it to be like that, but he had to realize all he'd dealt with were loose women. Stephanie had her own thoughts. They enjoyed the rest of their night together and made plans for the next day.

The next morning, they arose and went to breakfast. Stephanie was in awe, looking upon Jamaica in the daylight. She loved it and held on to Grant's arm as he escorted his wife around the hotel and restaurant. Later, they played racquetball for some exercise then went snorkeling. They took pleasure in their surroundings. They continued to "practice," and Stephanie was loosening up but still wasn't quite enjoying it. She could tell Grant was losing his luster to "help her out." It weighed heavy on him that he couldn't please his wife.

Meanwhile, Stephanie thought something was wrong with her. This whole sex thing was taking its toll. They were intoxicated and attracted to each other. It was a mystery why the sex wasn't bringing them closer together and instead seems to be stretching them apart.

For the rest of their honeymoon, they continued to enjoy the amenities instead of each other. Grant was feeling less than a man, and Stephanie was feeling less than a woman. When they returned home, Stephanie's best friend could tell there was something wrong with her. "Stephanie, you should be grinning from ear to ear. What's the matter, chick?" Arielya asked.

"You can't tell nobody, and I mean nobody about this," Stephanie said.

"I am sworn to secrecy," Arielya said.

"Grant and I had sex, but I'm not feelin' it, Arielya."

"What! Homeboy don't know what to do with it?"

"It's not that, Arielya."

"What is it then?"

"I don't know how it's supposed to feel. It hurts more so than anything. It has gotten a little better, but we didn't do it every day. I act like I have a headache and rollover."

"I know what you say he does, but what do you do?"

"Nothing because I don't know what to do. You know I don't know anything about sex, Arielya."

"Sounds like you need a little help."

"Uh, yeah, I do."

"I know you are a "church" girl and don't think about these things, but if you want to learn how to please your man, I have some websites you can go to."

"What you talkin' about 'Reilya?"

"There are books too. You don't have to be in the dark anymore. Girl, learn how to please your man."

"Are you talking about porn?"

"I don't see it like that. I see it as equipping myself with the "tools" I need to please my man."

"I ain't trying to be funny, but you ain't kept a man."

"I just haven't found the right one, Stephanie."

"I didn't mean anything by it, Arielya. I'm just saying your answers are not for me."

"Alright, but you better learn something from somewhere, or someone else will do what you too good to do."

"I guess."

Stephanie left her friend's house and went home to Grant's place. They were staying there until she moved to Jacksonville for good. She didn't want to stay there because things have been weird since their honeymoon, but of course, she couldn't tell him that, but he could tell she was running from him.

Grant decided to take matters into his own hands. Before Stephanie returned home, Grant put forth all his effort by setting the most perfect romantic atmosphere. Stephanie walked through the door, and he looked upon the beauty that was before him. The soft 90's R&B music captured her ears while the dimly lit living room drew her eyesight towards the blue and white rose petals going from the couch to the bedroom. When she saw all the trouble her husband went through, she gave into the atmosphere. Grant prepared a light dinner; pasta salad, herb-grilled salmon, dinner rolls, and freshly squeezed lemonade.

Stephanie quietly sat down, and Grant watched her sit in silence. Neither one spoke a word. Then he spread a linen napkin across his loins with one leg stretched across the couch and the other one on the edge and gestured for Stephanie to lay back in his lap. She scooted closer to him with a smile as he signaled. As soon as she did, Grant brought out the chocolate covered strawberries and began to feed them to her. Stephanie finally relaxed and let things happen. She wasn't tensed or timid. Grant could feel the calmness of the moment and wrapped his arm around her. He began kissing her on the neck. She laid back upon his chest and closed her eyes. She delighted in his kisses. Then Grant gently slid his fingers up and down her arms. Stephanie was in "heaven." As the four-play persisted, Grant picked up his wife and carried her to the bedroom. This night was the most passionate night they had since their honeymoon. Her body finally gave into his. This was the night that should have happened, the first night of their honeymoon.

After making love, Stephanie laid her head upon Grant's chest, and he held her in his arms. He asked her, "How are you feeling?"

"In love."

"Me too."

"Now I know how it's supposed to be. I know how it's supposed to feel."

"I don't think I'll ever understand why it was so hard for us."

"I'm not sure either; maybe it was because we put so much pressure on ourselves and each other to perform."

"True."

"Plus, the mood was right. All I really wanted was to be romanticized, and you did that, although I would have liked to eat the dinner that you cooked," she said, and they both laughed.

"I'll go get it."

"We can both go."

Stephanie wrapped herself in the sheets and headed out of the bedroom, and Grant did the same thing. They sat on the couch and fed each other. Once their bellies were full, they headed back to the activities that led them to hunger in the first place.

Chapter Six: Embarking on New Life

Grant and Stephanie's month is almost up, and it was time for her to start her new job. Grant drove her to Jacksonville and stayed with her for the weekend, but he had to be back to work on Monday.

Although Grant is saved now, he still loves science but keeps it in its place. He works in a research lab. His target is studying Autism. Grant gave Stephanie a kiss good-bye and said, "I will see you this weekend." Stephanie was nervous about starting this new career, and without the presence of her husband, it was much worse. She wasn't nervous about cooking but was about working with new people in a new place and leading the kitchen at Le Floures. Grant left to return to his place in Savannah while Stephanie prepared herself to start the next morning. Grant found it hard to leave her. They were finally connecting on all levels. She hated to see her husband go but knew this was coming. Therefore, she put on her big girl pants and marched on.

The night before she started work, Stephanie called her best friend, Arielya.

"Hey girl, how is it down there?" Arielya asked.

"It's good. I'm excited, but at the same time, I feel alone," Stephanie whined.

"Why?" Arielya asked.

"Because all that I know is far away from me. I can't pop up at your house. I can't stop by momma, and papa's whenever I want to," Stephanie said.

"True, but gurl quit whining about it. You made it out of the projects. That can't be said for a lot of us. I tell you what it couldn't be me. I would take that bull by the horns and ride baby," Arielya said.

"I know, but…"

"But what? Look, gurl, take this time to start your career and make a home for you and your husband and stop looking for something to complain about."

"Why are you so cold?"

"Because man, you got it made, don't have to suffer like the rest of us and you sittin' here whining. It's crazy. Obviously, you don't know what you have."

"I know what I have, but I just realized what I will be missing."

"What? Gunshots? Hoodrats? Watchin' your back, so you don't get robbed? Are you serious? Girl, bye, you better get real and leave that missing us mess alone."

"Well, I see I am not going to get anywhere with you. I will talk to you later."

After Stephanie hung up the phone with Arielya, she didn't call no one else. She thought long and hard about why her best friend acting crazy. She was shocked by Arielya's attitude. She was expecting her to say, "I know, girl, I miss you too! Come home and visit," but she didn't get any of that. Nevertheless, the more she thought about it, the madder she became but decided to let it go.

Stephanie prepared herself for work and laid down for the evening after having a short conversation with Grant. She arose the next morning, both excited and anxious. Although she's been cooking all her life, running a kitchen with people she doesn't know is a bit overwhelming. How will she be received? Are they still loyal to the last head-chef? Will they give her a hard time? Those are the questions that ailed her.

Grant called Stephanie before she went to work to pray with her and to tell her to take it one day at a time. He was so proud of his wife. Stephanie was grateful, and it calmed her nerves. She was ready to seize this great opportunity. She walked in, pressed, dressed, and ready. She was greeted by the restaurant owner, Tanner Godwin, saying, "Good morning Mrs. Bennet."

"Stephanie, sir. Good morning," she said, firmly shaking his hand.

"Alright, Stephanie, let me show you the kitchen," Tanner said.

"Sounds great," she said with a smile.

Tanner led her to the rest of the employees. He said, "Everyone, this is Stephanie, the new head-chef." They all responded with a friendly hello. Then Tanner continued, "Stephanie, the ones who will work with you in the kitchen is: Mannie, Richard, Jayla, and Sullivan. The waitresses you will work with are Tina, my daughter, Gretchen, Sunny, Tamiya, my other daughter, and the other ones you will meet later. My wife, Loren, is the house manager, and she will be in at 10 am."

"Nice to meet everyone," Stephanie said after taking a deep breath.

"Well, that's everyone. Now let's get to work," Tanner said.

"Is there anything you have for me?" Stephanie asked Tanner.

"I'm going to let all the waitresses go and prepare for the day while I talk to the kitchen staff and you," Tanner said.

"Okay," Stephanie answered.

"Do you have any questions, Stephanie?" Tanner asked.

"Yes, I would like to ask them something," Stephanie said, hinting towards those that work in the kitchen.

"Dawg," Mannie said. Tanner cut his eye at him.

"How did the last head-chef run the kitchen?" she asked them.

"He didn't, and that's why he isn't here anymore," Mannie answered.

"There had to be something he did right. What were the things he did that you did like?" She asked the team.

Stephanie continued to ask the team about the last chef, but none had anything nice to say about him. She tried not to let on, but she was nervous and scared to take over. She spent her first day learning the kitchen and how things ran.

After she got off work, the first thing she did was call her mother on the phone.

"Hello," said Mrs. Chase as she answered the phone.

"Hey, momma. How are you doing?" Stephanie asked.

"Missing my baby girl," said Mrs. Chase.

"Oh, momma," Stephanie said.

"It sounds like my baby is missing home too. What's going on?" Mrs. Chase asked.

"You always know when something is wrong with me," Stephanie said.

"Yes, I do," Mrs. Chase said.

"Momma, I'm scared. When I went to work today, I was overwhelmed."

"Why?"

"It's like I walked into a kitchen for the first time. I even asked them about the last chef and how he ran things, but they didn't have anything good to say about him, so I'm still at square one."

"Oh, okay, I see what your problem is. Stephanie, just think about it like this; you know how we ran the kitchen at home?"

"Yes, ma'am."

"It's the same thing. When you go into work tomorrow, own it. Make it work to your advantage and how you feel comfortable. Then add all the technical things to running a kitchen you learned in school."

"Thanks, momma. I didn't look at it like that. I wish Grant were here because maybe I wouldn't be so nervous."

"Hopefully, he won't be away too long. How is the job market down there?"

"I don't know. Can't be too good because he's been looking but nothing."

"Baby, you know the words of prayer, use them."

"Yes, ma'am."

"Well, baby, I have to go. Daddy and I are going out on a date."

"Alright now. Behave yourself."

"I don't have to behave. I'm grown." Mrs. Chase said; then they laughed as they ended their conversation.

The next day, Stephanie went into the restaurant and owned the place after following her mother's advice. She became the natural cook she is and confident. Her fellow co-workers liked the way she worked the kitchen. She figured the guy before her must have been rough because the kitchen staff worked easy with her.

As the week went by, Stephanie was getting excited to see her husband. All she could remember is the night of bliss, and she was looking forward to another blissful evening.

Despite Stephanie's great week, Grant ended up with a horrible one. The clinical trial research at the biotech center for Autism he managed hit a dead end. Plus, he barely talked with his wife this week. He couldn't see himself leaving his work unfinished, so he had to make a call he really didn't want to make. Grant misses his wife and knows this isn't going to go over well, but what can he do?

"Hey baby," Stephanie said, answering Grant's phone call.

"Hey there, sexy lady," Grant said.

"How was your day?"

"It wasn't good at all, Steph. How was yours?"

"Actually, it turned out to be pretty alright."

"I'm glad it's turning out good for you."

"It means nothing because I can't see you. I can't wait for you to come up this weekend."

"About that…," Grant began to say.

"When are you leaving?"

"Steph, that's what I want to talk to you about."

"If you have to come a little later, that's fine, just as long as you get here."

"Baby, I'm not…"

"Don't finish that sentence. Have you not noticed that I keep ignoring you?"

"Yes, I do, and that's what makes this so hard, but sweetheart, I'm not going to be able to make it."

"Why not, Grant?"

"This week was rough. You know I've been working on an assignment for the past few months. I've got all the data together and preparing the information for the contributors who are coming next week. Well, it all came crashing down, and I have to figure out what went wrong and get it done before they get here."

"Is there anything I can do to help?"

"Stephanie, be real, what can you do?"

"What's that supposed to mean?"

"Nothing. Look, I appreciate what you are trying to do, but it's not going to work. I miss you and want nothing more than to be there with you, but I have to get this done. You know how important this research is to me."

"I know how important it is to you. I'm sure your sister loves what you're doing as she looks down on you. And not taking anything from that, but I don't see how not coming up here will make things any better. Maybe you just need to relax. You can work things out better when your mind is clear."

"Easier said than done. I have to get back to work. I will call you this weekend, okay."

"Is this how you really want to end the conversation?"

"Steph, don't make it out to be more than what it is."

"How else am I supposed to take it?"

"You are way too emotional."

"Yeah, okay, this conversation is over. All I want is to see you, and if that's too emotional, then so be it."

"Need you talk? We wouldn't be in this situation if…never mind."

"Yep! Never mind. I can't believe you would bring that back up, ugh!" Stephanie said as she hung up the phone.

"Step…," Grant tried to say.

Grant attempted to call Stephanie time and time again, but she refused to answer. She was furious with him. He stopped worrying about it and went back to work, and she decided to get with her new boss to see if she could work extra hours for the weekend. She figured since she wasn't going to see her husband, she might as well work.

The weekend came and went and without either of them speaking to each other, not by choice. Grant was the only one trying to resolve the situation and called his wife on numerous occasions, but she wouldn't answer the phone. She was busy working hard the whole weekend to get her mind off her husband.

Grant found it difficult to work because he couldn't stand the tension between him and Stephanie. After making some leeway with the testing and some minor connections while working with his colleagues, he decided to surprise his wife by visiting her. He made his arrangements and set out to be in their apartment by the time his wife comes home from work.

Stephanie made the necessary changes at work for the kitchen to flow efficiently. The staff could sense that something wasn't right with her.

Inwardly, Stephanie was crumbling inside because she knew she had overreacted with the whole situation. She wants the best for her husband and knows how he feels about his work, especially since his whole purpose is to help those like his sister, Adriana. How she behaved was unacceptable and not very Christian like. She watched her parents as she grew up and never saw her mother disrespect her father at any time; therefore knew she was out of line.

It's around 6:45 pm, and she is on her way home from work. She was tired because she had been there since 5 am and worked late. Stephanie was ready to get home and call her husband to apologize.

Meanwhile, she didn't know that Grant called to see when she was getting off work. He wanted everything to be ready when she came home. Stephanie was getting ready to walk through the door to the biggest surprise.

She came through the door but didn't notice anything. Grant set it up that way. She went into the bedroom, took off her work clothes, and prepared for a hot shower. She noticed a light coming from her bathroom with soft music playing in the background. Stephanie walked very carefully to the door, opened it cautiously, and when she peeked around the door, she was floored. Stephanie saw lit scented candles, dimmed lights, heard R&B soul music playing with a sexy, hot man with nothing on except light faded blue jeans sitting beside the bathtub. He brought a huge smile on her face. Grant stood up, gently finished undressing his beautiful wife, and put her in the hot and soapy bathtub. She laid back and closed her eyes as he soaked the water up with a towel and draped it across her neck to where the water trickled down her body. She opened her eyes and stared at her husband. He caught her looking at him and gave her the sexiest smile. His smile always makes her heart melt. And before she knew it, in a calm voice, she said, "Grant, I'm sorry about how I acted."

"Ssh," Grant said.

She grabbed the finger he used to hush her up, looked intently into his eyes, and said, "No, I have to say this. I have caused you pain, then expected you to just live with it, and that's wrong. I'm sorry, Grant. You've been good to me and did not deserve the way I treated you. I know how important your work is to you, and I should have respected that. I acted like a child. I'm sorry."

"Thank you, babe. I'm sorry too. I never should have brought the past back up. Let's just move past it and enjoy the evening."

"How long are you here for?"

"I don't have to be back to work until Monday."

"But it's Thursday, won't that be too long?"

"While you work tomorrow, I'm going to drive back home. It's only a two-hour drive. I'm going to work for a while, then head back down. But don't worry your pretty little head about it. I have it all under control."

"I guess you are the top dog, huh?"

"You know I run thangs," Grant said as they laughed.

"So you mean to tell me all I have to do is act up, and you'll drive down here? Hmm…"

"Don't get any ideas."

After they laughed, a comfortable silence flowed through the atmosphere. Stephanie asked, "So are you going to let me stay in this bathtub all by myself, or are you going to join me?"

"What do you want me to do?"

"Whatever you want me to."

"I like the sound of that."

The next morning, Stephanie got up to head out to work. She was going in as a different woman, a happy one. The fact that Grant will be there when she gets home from work makes her day worthwhile. Grant woke up and headed back to Savannah. He did as he said he would do, then drove back to Jacksonville but sent in resumes as well. He didn't want to be away from his wife for months on end.

They took the time to enjoy each other and to reconnect. It was something they needed to do because they allowed so much to come between them. Stephanie realized how big of a mistake she made by taking this job without telling Grant. She understood fully the implications of her actions now. It's not that she didn't know before, but the stress of the consequence of her decision is evident. Stephanie figured this was going to take some work, but Grant is worth it.

Sunday rolled around, and it was time for Grant to leave. Neither one wanted to let go. It was hard to do this a second time. She wasn't sure if she could keep this up. Nevertheless, she's willing to do what she has it to make it work.

Chapter Seven: Hard Places

Over the next eight months, Grant and Stephanie visited each other as much as possible, but it put a strain on their marriage. As time went by, they saw less and less of each other, although they often talked on the phone.

Grant worked hard to debunk the information he received that made him feel like he hit a dead end. Finally, after some time, Grant's clinical trial research for Autism became lucrative for the bio lab. His research was gaining momentum, and he could be close with new and exciting information about Autism. He earned a lot of recognition, such as a promotion, a generous amount of money donated to the program from contributors, highlighted in the news abroad, and his own story in a science magazine. He didn't win over Mr. Bannaker, who doesn't like the side effects and whose contribution would take this clinical study over the top. Even though he has the respect of fellow scientists and contributors, and investors, it's still not enough to give the clinical research the backing it needs.

In addition, a graduate student named Ashley Stephenson is working on a documentary about Grant, his clinical theory, and why finding a cure for autism vital to him. She has followed him around for the past six months. They became close, and one big main reason why Grant no longer wanted to visit his wife on the weekends.

Stephanie's career started coming between them because of the long work hours and a slave paycheck. She couldn't get the time off despite

Grant's constant begging. She hadn't even been to church. Mr. and Mrs. Chase made sure they kept Grant focused on church to keep him on track. They noticed the young lady Ashley was around Grant all the time. It made them a little suspicious, and Mr. Chase decided to speak with Grant about it.

Mr. Chase headed over to Grant's one late afternoon. He figured Grant would be home from work by that time. He knocked on the door, and to his surprise, Ashley answered.

"Hello, Mr. Chase. Come on in," Ashley said.

"Oh, I'm sorry, I'm looking for Grant," Mr. Chase said confused.

"Yes, sure, he's here. We were just finishing up the taping," she said.

"Oh, how is the documentary coming along?" Mr. Chase asked.

"Really well. Grant is brilliant, and his contributions to the scientific field are phenomenal," Ashley said.

Grant walked into the living room and said, "Thank you, Ashley, but there are others whose contributions are just as great as mine."

"Yeah, I know, but this is about you," she said.

He smiled, then walked over to his father-in-law and said, "It's good to see you. What brings you this way?"

"I just wanted to talk with my favorite son-in-law," Mr. Chase said.

"Well, I'm going to go. I'll see you tomorrow at your office?" Ashley asked.

"Sure, I'll be there," Grant said. Ashley said goodbye to Mr. Chase and winked at Grant.

"Come on and have a seat, dad," Grant said. Then he went to the kitchen and fixed him and Mr. Chase a glass of sweet tea. "Here you go," Grant said handing Mr. Chase the glass.

"Thank you," Mr. Chase said.

"What's on your mind? You look a little disturbed."

"I am."

"Why? What's wrong?"

"Why is that young lady in your apartment?"

"You know, dad. She's filming me for the documentary."

"So, you don't see a problem with being in an apartment alone with a young lady, and you're married? She's too comfortable; she's answering your door for Christ's sake. What if that was Stephanie at the door? How do you think she would have taken that?"

"Stephanie knows Ashley and wouldn't have made a big deal about it."

Mr. Chase looked at Grant, shook his head, and said, "Son, I thought you knew my daughter."

"I do."

"Not if you think she would have been fine with that. Please remember, Stephanie is from the projects. She may seem sweet but cross her, and you'll see a side you've never seen before."

"Not Steph. She's too mature for all that."

"You're naïve. Don't sleep on, baby girl. That's all I'm going to tell you."

"The thing is we're not doing anything wrong."

"She likes you, and I can see it."

"Who? Ashley? Noooo. This is strictly professional."

"I'm not sure she knows that, and I'm beginning to wonder if you know that yourself."

"Dad, you have nothing to worry about because I'd never do anything to hurt my wife."

"Thing is, no one ever intends on hurting someone they love. It's never done purposely, but they end up doing so because they don't put their flesh in check. Don't think it can't happen to you."

"Never. I'm in love with my wife, regardless of what we go through. I'm the one doing all the calling and begging her to come home, but she keeps saying she can't make it. Stephanie has missed every award ceremony and publicity engagement, and she barely calls me."

"You need to tell her how you feel. Y'all need to talk about this; otherwise, you are going to find yourself in a compromising position that could cost you your marriage."

"Dad, Mr. Chase, I don't want Ashley. I don't even see her in that way. I want my wife, and she is all I need."

"Okay, son. I wanted to talk to you about it because last time we saw y'all together, there looked to be a lot of flirting going on between the both of you."

"Be rest assured, dad, that will never happen."

They continued to talk and watch television for a little bit then Mr. Chase left to go home.

Meanwhile, Mrs. Chase tried calling her daughter to warn her about Ashley and give her a few wifely tips, but she couldn't reach her. Even though Stephanie took classes at church about preparing for marriage, there were some things it just didn't teach her. She's been out of church for so long the teachings she learned seem far away. She has been in church all her life, and now she's barely graced the door with her presence. She got so wrapped up in her career that she laid God to the side along with her husband.

A few weeks later, Grant called Stephanie, whom he hadn't talked to in three days, only to hear the words, "I can't come home because I'm working this weekend." He hadn't seen his wife going on two months and had been asking for her to come home just as long. She missed all his publicity engagements except for one due to her hours at work. He tried to explain that Ashley wanted to talk with her for the documentary, but she continued to let him know she couldn't make it home but would speak with her on the phone. She spoke with Ashley on this day and answered all her questions. Stephanie didn't pick up on the accolades Ashley was giving Grant. She was clueless.

Once they ended the phone conversation, Ashley noticed Grant was looking a little down and asked him, "Are you okay?"

"Yeah, I'm cool," he answered.

"Awh, come on, Grant. For the past few weeks, you haven't been yourself. I would think you'd be ecstatic with all the publicity you've been getting."

"You noticed, huh?"

"It's hard not to; I mean, we've been working side by side for some time now."

"At least you noticed."

"You miss her, don't you?"

"Of course, she is my wife."

"Hey, I got the perfect thing to get your mind off of things."

"I don't do that."

"Do what? I'm talking about good food."

"I'm not sure that's wise."

She grabbed Grant by the hand, pulled him up from his couch, and said, "Come on! You've got to eat."

They went to a quaint little restaurant. Grant liked it and enjoyed himself. The conversation was quite nice. He hadn't been in his wife's company in a while, and conversation was just about nonexistent. He laughed, smiled, and didn't think about Stephanie once.

After eating a lovely meal and having a great conversation, they left the restaurant, and Grant drove Ashley to her apartment. She asked him to come in for coffee, but he declined. She said, "Okay. See you tomorrow," then kissed him on the cheek and got out of the car. He watched her walk into her apartment building then drove off once she went inside.

A few minutes later, Ashley answered a knock at her door. It was Grant. She couldn't believe he was standing there, and neither could he. Grant said, "If the offer is still on the table, I would like a cup of coffee." She didn't say anything, just opened the door and gestured for him to enter. As soon as he walked in, she headed to the kitchen and brewed some coffee. He sat down on the couch quietly. She headed for the sofa and sat next to him after turning on the television.

She swung her hair to the side and asked him, "How's your coffee?"

"It's fine," he answered as he watched the show.

"I didn't know how much sugar to put in it because I don't know how you like your coffee."

"It could use a little more sugar, but it's good. I'm not a heavy coffee drinker anyway."

"I can add some sugar."

"Don't worry about it."

She took her pointer finger, placed it on his cheek, and turned his head towards her, and said, "But I want to add something sweet to your life." Then she kissed him, and he did not turn away or try to stop it from happening. She began kissing him on his neck. At first, he didn't move, then later gave in to temptation. This started a three-month affair. Grant felt guilty every single time, and after three months, he ended it because he loved his wife. Ashley didn't like it one bit. She vowed to get him back. Grant was upfront with her the whole time, letting her know that he wasn't leaving his wife for her. Ashley took it hard. Grant couldn't keep walking into church, knowing he was having an affair. He had to get things right. He suffered condemnation and went before God and repented but kept it a secret from his wife. He figured the best thing to do was to quit his job and move instantly to Jacksonville, FL with Stephanie. He couldn't believe he let things get this far, and this bad before he decided to move. It was then he remembered the words of his father-in-law, "No one ever intends on hurting someone they love. Don't think it can't happen to you."

Stephanie wondered what the sudden change of heart was about, but she was happy to have her husband in the place they could call their own. She decided to make some changes at the restaurant and asked her boss if she could hire a sous chef to help take the load off her, and he concurred.

Following the move to Florida, Grant stayed away from Stephanie as much as possible because he didn't want her to get too close. Grant was distant, and Stephanie didn't know why, but he pushed her away in the process. He wouldn't sleep with her, nor would he kiss her on the lips, only on her forehead. Her husband was different but could only attribute it to being apart for so long. She made advances only to be rejected. She tried setting up times to go out on dates, but he didn't accept. He stopped doing things to woo her. She thought to herself, "I have to do something to get him to love me again."

Over time, she began to think something was wrong with her. The words of her best friend started to ring in her ear, "I know you are a "church" girl and don't think about these things, but if you want to learn how to please your man, I have some websites you can go to."

Later one evening, when she came home from work, Stephanie waited for Grant to go to sleep. She went on the computer and typed in something as simple as how to please your man sexually. A whirlwind of porn websites came up; not medical or clean versions, not anything really helpful. She went to all kinds of sites and watched all sorts of things, and nothing she'd ever done with Grant would come up on the screen. She felt inadequate and surely was the reason her husband wouldn't lay with her. She said to herself, "This must be what the other girls did that he dated. I just don't measure up. I can't compete with this." She took notes, and over the next couple of months, she regularly watched sites and tried to imitate what the women were doing.

Stephanie was determined to win over her husband. The next few "sexcapades" Grant submitted to blew his mind but wondered where his wife learned these new moves. He thought in his head, "I'm mean, she was a virgin up until we got married. Has she been cheating on me?" It left many questions in his head, and he barely wanted to participate because of these reasons. Still, he dare not approach her with it because that would mean that he would have to face his sin. However, through all of that, the things she did in bed with him still didn't please him. Grant was more pleased with his wife before all the "extras."

The next morning after another "sexcapade," Grant asked his wife if she could take off work and spend the day with him. She called in sick to spend the day with her husband. Grant had something in mind when he asked his wife to do this and needed some questions answered. It wasn't intimate or just spending time with her; it was for his own personal gain. As they sat at the table for breakfast, Grant asked, "What have you been up to lately?"

"What do you mean?"

"You haven't been yourself lately."

"I could say the same about you."

"What do you mean?"

"Nothing."

"Stephanie, there's no easy way to say this."

"Then, just say it."

"I was on the computer the other day searching for more places for me to put in my resume and…"

"And?"

"And some websites popped up that I know for certain I haven't been on." Stephanie shuddered on the inside because, over time, she became addicted to watching porn. She enjoyed watching it more than performing it. She started out watching porn to learn how to please her husband like Arielya told her to, but now she watches it for her own enjoyment. She'd replace Grant with porn and was satisfied with the satisfaction of masturbation. She trembled to ask him where he was going with these questions, but she asked anyway, "Okay…where are you going with this?"

"I'm just going to ask. have you been on porn sites?"

"You know I don't watch porn."

"Well then, where did you get those moves from? Are you cheating on me?"

"What moves? Cheating? Are you crazy?"

"Don't play stupid. You know our sex has been different; not that I'm complaining, but it's not you. I want you in our bed, not somebody else."

"The only thing I've done is read some books," Stephanie said, realizing she's lying to her husband.

"Why would you have to read books?"

"Grant, when you moved here, you were so distant. You wouldn't touch me, not even kiss me."

"I did kiss you."

"Yeah, you kissed me on the forehead as if I was a child. You made me feel worthless. On top of that, you turned me down every time I came on to you. I didn't know why you wouldn't have sex with me. You can only reject a person so many times. So, I figured, maybe I could read some books, and maybe that could help, and low and behold, it did."

Trying to deflect the blame back on her so he wouldn't have to answer for his own wrongdoings, he looked at her and said, "Reject. That's funny coming from you because how many times did I ask you to come to see me, attend events with me, just spend time with me, and you always turned me down."

"I was working. It wasn't because I didn't want to come and see you but look at our bills. We were running two households and not a lot of money to do it with, so yes, I chose to work instead of coming up to visit you."

"I needed you, and I felt like you turned your back on me."

"Grow up. We got grown folk bills with high school money. You know I didn't turn my back on you. If anything, I was helping to take the load off your back."

"I see this is getting us nowhere."

"And I can't believe I took off work for this," Stephanie said as she got up from the breakfast table, grabbed her keys, and left the apartment. She ran so she wouldn't have to answer any more of his questions about what was on the computer.

He said, "Yeah, do what you do best, run." Grant concluded that even though his wife was hiding watching porn, he knew he was the reason she was doing this and remembering his own sin. He stopped inquiring because it would only lead back to him. Then he thought, "I won't be able to live with myself if I let this keep going. She doesn't deserve this." He went after her and caught her on the stairs, snatched the keys from her, and said,

"Come on back upstairs. You're going to stop running every time things get hard." She absolutely hated that he was right. Once they got back upstairs and into their apartment, he said to his wife, "I'm sorry, Stephanie. I didn't mean to make you feel like that. I have a lot of pressure on me. My wife is supporting me, and I don't like that. I am a man, and I have to pull my own weight."

"Grant, you will find a job. Plus, you made good money while you were there, but we just couldn't see any of it because of running two households. However, we have a nice little nest egg set up. I'm not supporting you, so don't say that. We have enough that should hold us over until you find a new job."

"I know, but Stephanie, listen, on another subject, here me when I say, I don't want another woman in the bed with me. I want my wife, and I want to be the one to teach her what she wants to know, not to have her learn it from a book."

"Didn't have a choice because you weren't teaching me anything."

"I know, and I'm sorry, and that's going to change."

"Let me ask you a question, though?"

"Shoot."

"Why did you all of a sudden decide to move here without a job, anyway?"

"I just couldn't be away from you any longer, Steph. I started having doubts and questioning our marriage because we hadn't seen each other in a while then was hardly talking on the phone. Our marriage couldn't take much more. I…I just…felt like I was losing you."

"But why? I know my schedule was hectic, but you had to know my love didn't change for you."

"How was I supposed to know when you wouldn't even return my calls. It didn't seem like you supported me. It was all about you and your job."

"Really? Really Grant? I mean, seriously, you have to think about it, I am running a kitchen and crew. It's not a walk in the park. You have no idea what I do, do you?"

"Steph, you're just cookin'."

She pauses for a second and said, "Just cooking? Spoken like a true person who doesn't have a clue how a kitchen runs. I bet you don't even know how many chefs end up on drugs and alcohol because of the stress. Families get ripped apart, debt is certain, fights between employees, and the turnover labor is horrendous because there isn't enough money in the budget to pay them with what they deal with daily. Then to have to deal with the ignorance of customers, such as yourself, who think they're better than them while not knowing the mechanics and logistics of running a restaurant. So, no, it's not just cooking."

"I didn't mean to offend you, Steph. I was just being honest."

"So, how would you feel if I said you're wasting your time with your clinical trials for autism? People waste their time giving you their money because the government will not allow a cure to be made public even if you discover one. I mean, I'm just being honest," she said as she sarcastically shrugged her shoulders.

Grant looked at her like he wanted to throw her against the wall. "Why would you say something like that when you know how important this research is to me?"

"And you know how important being a chef is to me. You don't like how it feels, then don't do it to me. Of course, I don't believe that for one second. I believe in what you do, even though you don't believe in my dream."

"I do, Steph."

"No, you don't because if you did, then "just cooking" wouldn't have come out your mouth. Don't worry about it, though. It's cool, but it ain't gone stop me cause I'm going to have my own restaurant one day, and it's going to be because I believed in myself."

That night, Stephanie wouldn't allow Grant to sleep in the bed with her. He slept on the couch. She found herself surfing the internet in the late-night hours, checking her social networks, then became bored and eventually fell asleep.

After a while, she low-key started arguments with him to have an excuse to "surf" the web. She went on the websites her husband had questioned her about only a few weeks ago. She knew it was wrong, but she didn't care. She hadn't been in church for a while, and everything her parents instilled in her was fading away. Things with Grant was so intense porn became her escape. Stephanie went to different sites and discovered herself masturbating even more and immensely enjoying it.

One night after arguing with Stephanie, Grant slept on the couch, and he picked up his phone to call Ashley. He was thinking of going to visit her. He figured there was no need to keep arguing with one person when another woman wants to be with him. "Mmm…hey, I knew you'd be back," Ashley said, answering Grant's phone call. "I didn't think I would, but I guess you know better than I do," Grant said. "What's wrong? I can tell something is bothering you," Ashley said. "I'm just tired of all the arguing. It's old," said Grant. "Well, I'm here, and I'm not arguing. I just want you," Ashley said. "When can I come to see you?" Grant whispered on the phone, so Stephanie wouldn't hear him. "Anytime. I will clear my schedule for you," Ashley said. "I'll be there this weekend," Grant said. "I'll see you then," Ashley responded, then hung up the phone.

Throughout the night, while he was sleeping on the couch, Grant tossed and turned because the dreams of his adultery tormented him. Nothing he tried to do to get comfortable worked. He was restless. Finally, he decided to get up and see if he could fix things with his wife. She heard his footsteps and quickly exited out of the site she was on and opened her social media handles as the doorknob twisted open. He looked at her as she watched him come through the door.

"What are you doing?" Grant asked.

"Just surfing my social media sites," she answered.

"Look, Stephanie, I am tired of all this arguing. Either we are going to do this marriage thing or not; what's it gone be?"

"You're tired of arguing, yet you come up in here with an ultimatum? No apologies. No, let's fix this. Just, we gone do this or not. Doesn't sound like you want to be here to me."

"That's not what I meant. All I'm saying is, can we get past all of this and get back to us?"

"I want that too, but it really hurts to know you don't believe in me."

"You're still on that? Babe, I apologized to you about that weeks ago."

"I know, but I just feel like you don't."

"What do I have to do to prove to you I do believe in you?"

"I don't know. You'll find a way if you choose to."

He sat down on the bed and held her hands and said, "Sweetheart, can we start over, please? I don't want to fight anymore."

"Me neither. So, how do we get past this?"

"Come on. Get up. Let's get out of this apartment for a while. How about we go home this weekend."

"That'll work cause I got this weekend off."

Grant and Stephanie got up, got dressed, then went for a nice walk around the apartment complex. It was already late at night, and since nothing was open, they decided to walk and talk, holding hands. After about 45 minutes of walking around the neighborhood, they headed back to their place. Upon arriving at their apartment, Stephanie took out her key. She began to put the key in the lock, then Grant turned her around, pinned her against the wall, and said, "Can I have a kiss goodnight before you go." Playing along with his seduction, she said, "You wouldn't have to do that if you stayed the night."

He said, "Are you asking me to spend the night?"

She said, "My bed is yours."

"Well, can I have a preview of what's to come?"

Stephanie didn't say a word; she slipped her hands under his shirt to reach his belt buckle as she kissed him. He kissed her back while turning the key to unlock the door. He stopped her kisses, twirled her around towards the door, and said, "After you." As they kissed after the door slammed shut and Grant touching Stephanie all over her body, she began to see flashes of the porn she'd watch. It was no longer about her and Grant. It was about her, the porn, her pleasures, then Grant. She became more turned on as their loving went on through the night. It was as if she almost needed these scene flashes to get her to a place of pleasure. Now it wasn't up to Grant to pleasure her; it was up to porn.

Afterward, they turned towards one another, talking lying in bed together. Then Grant said something that would completely change the mood, he said, "Let's go to church Sunday with your parents when we go home this weekend."

This caught Stephanie off guard. She hasn't been in only God knows how long and felt like she couldn't go back after being involved with porn, plus her pastor can read folk like a book, and that frightened her. Her sin will be found out, so she came up with an excuse, "I have things to do Sunday before going back to work on Monday."

"Like what?"

"I have to work on the schedule, inventory, and ordering products."

"Does that take a lot of time?"

"It can, especially the inventory, because I have to do a check before I can order more product. Church can take up a lot of time, and I don't want to get back here late and then have to be up early to be at work by five in the morning."

"Yeah, but two hours away. It's not a long drive."

"Can we just leave in the morning to come back home? I want to be able to do what I got to do and relax and rest before heading back into a heavy work schedule."

"This time, cause I miss going to church with you, babe."

"I know, but we will again and soon. I promise," she found herself saying but knowing she had no intent on going to church.

"I hope so," he said as he kissed his wife. Stephanie went to sleep. She knew she was already going to be exhausted at work tomorrow because she has to be there by 7 AM, and it was already three in the morning. Grant held her while she slept. He still couldn't sleep. He had a lot on his mind. He just made a date with a woman he had an affair with, then made up with his wife. He also lingered on the thoughts of the day when she would go to church with him.

Meanwhile, lying in bed restless, he decided to get up and grab him something small to eat. Before he left the room, he made sure Stephanie was all tucked in. However, he tripped over her laptop on the floor by her dresser. He stared at it for a while, wondering if this would be a good time to scan Stephanie's laptop to see what she's been watching. Grant was conflicted for a minute because he felt like he should believe what his wife told him, but on the other hand, he knew better; he had a gut feeling that she wasn't telling the truth. After tossing the idea back and forth, Grant decided to leave it alone. It's too late at night to deal with foolishness, so he went ahead and picked it up off the floor and headed to the kitchen. Eventually, Grant finally went to bed.

The weekend was upon them, and they headed down to Savannah, GA, to visit their family. Mr. & Mrs. Chase was happy to see their daughter. They hadn't seen or talked to her in a while. Stephanie used her job as an excuse to run from everything and everybody. They all went out to eat for lunch, laughed, talked, catching up on what's been going on in their lives. Then Grant and Stephanie went to go see his mother for a while, then she left so they could catch up while she went to go see Arielya. While Grant was visiting with his mother, Ashley called. "Give me a sec, mama; I have to take this." She excused him but wondered why he would have to step away to take a phone call. She knew that feeling all too well. He stepped outside to take the call. Meanwhile, his mother hid behind the door to hear his conversation.

"Hello," Grant said, answering the phone.

"Hey handsome, when are you coming to see me?" Ashley asked.

"I can't."

"What do you mean you can't?"

"I never should have called you. Me and Steph worked things out," he said. His mother put her head down because her suspicions were right, and she was disappointed in her son.

"What does that have to do with me," Ashley said, responding to Grant.

"I shouldn't have involved you. I'm sorry."

"Don't be. Either you come to see me, or I come to see you."

Grant hesitated. He didn't want any problems, and he really didn't want Stephanie to find out. He said, "Alright, just give me a minute to get there."

"Okay. See you in a few," she said as she hung up. Ashley went and put on a sexy negligee, her seductive smell goods, and primped her hair just the way Grant likes as she waited for his arrival.

When they hung up the phone, Grant walked back into the house, not realizing his mother heard his conversation. He asked her, "Mama, can I use your car to make a quick run?"

She looked at her son and said, "A quick run? Won't Stephanie be back in a little bit?"

"I told her I'd call her when I was ready."

"Grant, don't be like your father."

"What are you talking about?"

"Sit down."

"But mama, I gotta…"

"Sit."

"Yes, ma'am."

"I never told you, boys, why your father and I split up."

"It was because of Adriana."

"Adriana was just the straw that broke the camel's back."

"What do you mean? Y'all were so happy."

"It seemed that way to you and your brothers because I wasn't going to allow y'all to see how broken our marriage was."

"Why are you telling me this now, mama?"

"Just listen and take from it what you will. Do you remember all those business trips your father went on?"

"Yes."

"All of them were not business trips. The company your father worked for caused him to travel often but not as often as he had me to think. I always had my suspicions but couldn't prove anything until the company called to see if he could come into work to handle something important that had come up. I was speechless. Imagine how I felt having to tell them I thought he was already on a business trip. It opened an investigation, and it turns out he was using company funds to take these women on trips. He was taking women on these expensive trips and spending the weekend with them. I caught him three different times. I forgave each time, but the last time took me out. I couldn't do it anymore. He lost his job. Then the loss of Adriana and dealing with her death on my own while he spent time with another woman and the kids he had with her..."

"What!"

"Yes, your father had a whole nother family. I had to make all Adriana's funeral arrangements by myself while he played daddy to them, bastards."

"You mean to tell me I have other brothers or sisters?"

"Yes, you do."

"Why didn't you tell me?"

"I could give a damn about her and them bastard kids. That's your father's story to tell. I wasn't going to put y'all through that kind of pain. You already had a hard time when we split up, so think about how you would have flipped if I would have told you about that. Don't ask me about them cause I don't know anything and don't care to know. If you want to know more, then you will have to ask your father."

Grant was fuming. He said, "I need some air. Where are your keys?"

"They're hanging on the rack by the door like always."

"I'll be back, mama."

"Grant."

"Yes, mama."

"Don't make Stephanie feel like how your father made me feel."

He paused and looked at her, then said, "Mama, I gotta go." He slammed the door and got in her car. He called Stephanie to let her know he would be a while because of what his mom just told him, and he needed to be by himself to think. She tried to say that she would come to get him to talk about it but insisted he wanted to be alone. She gave him his space, although she was worried about him. He hung up with her and texted Ashley to let her know that he's on his way.

While he drove from the southside of Savannah to Pooler, thoughts ran through his head a million miles a minute. He had no clue all that went on between his parents. Things started to click though, and why he was no longer around after their marriage was dissolved. Still, he never even gave thought to his father having outside children. That took the cake. He couldn't think straight. He thought he was over all his parent's drama, and this sent him back into the abyss of his past. He turned into the apartment complex, parked, took a deep breath, and headed up the steps to see Ashley. He rang the doorbell. When she opened the door, he saw this young, sexy, vibrant woman playing the 2000's R&B music, who had her apartment lightly dimmed and scented lavender candles lit. Ashely knew if she could relax his mind, she could have his soul. Grant immediately thought to himself, "And Stephanie talking about can we talk about it when this is what I need. She doesn't ever do stuff like this."

Then Ashley said, snapping him back into reality, "Don't just stand there. Come on in, handsome," as she pulled him close to her by his shirt. He said, "You look amazing." "Anything to make you smile," Ashley said. He wasted no time kissing her. Grant picked her up in his arms as she wrapped her legs around his waist. As soon as she did that, the memory of Stephanie zoomed across his thoughts to the first time she did that when they were engaged. It made him stop in his tracks. He shook his head to snap out of it, then Ashley asked him, "Is everything alright?" He replied to her question but nodding his head yes. They went back to getting it on, and as they headed to her bedroom kissing, he heard, "Is this what you really want to do? Is this how you want to handle things?" He stopped again for a second then continued on because nothing would stop how he was feeling. As he laid her on her bed, he could hear the last words his mother said to him, "Don't make Stephanie feel like how your father made me feel." He felt like he was at a crossroads; if he continued, there would be no turning back, but he could save himself if he stopped now. They were almost fully undressed, just short of their unmentionables, and Grant said, "I can't do this." Ashley kept trying to entice him, but he got up, got dressed, and left. He told her that he loves his wife, and he never should have put her in the middle of their issues. He apologized to her and left. Ashley was confused about what just happened, but he saved himself. Since Grant's phone call earlier that week, he wasn't aware that Ashley skipped her birth control pills. Her plan was to ruin Grant's marriage by any means necessary.

Consequently, he was headed down the same path as his father and didn't even know it. He ran back to his mother's house. When he got there, he asked his mother to drop him off at his in-laws. He knew he had to get Ashley's scent off him before he could be around Stephanie. His mother could smell the scent of the other woman on him and didn't even bother to ask if he did it or not. The scent told her all she needed to know. Once they pulled up to the in-laws, Grant looked at his mom and said, "Mama, I didn't go through with it. I almost did, but I changed my mind." She said, "I'm glad you made the right choice. I know it couldn't have been easy." He said, "At first it wasn't, but when I heard your voice in my head, it became easy." His mother said, "I love you, son. You all have a safe trip home." He gave his mother a hug and told her he loves her and left. When he went inside, his in-laws were sitting on the couch watching television. "Where's Stephanie?" Mrs. Chase asked. "She's with Arielya," Grant answered. "Lawd, when them two get together, help us all," said Mrs. Chase. "Right!" Grant said, and they all laughed. He headed to the bathroom to get a shower and change into his pajamas. He texted his wife to let her know that he's back at her parent's place and he'll see her when she gets back. He hid the clothes he wore in the gym bag they brought with them.

Stephanie arrived at her parent's place about an hour later. When she came in, she saw everybody sitting on the couch, watching television and laughing, so she followed suit. He told her to go and get her shower and get relaxed to spend time with her parents before leaving in the morning. Stephanie did just that. After a while, they all headed to bed. Stephanie told Grant that it was a good idea to visit home. She enjoyed herself and precisely what she needed to wind down, stop, and take a breather. It felt good to be home. Grant felt the total opposite and was ready to get back to their own home in Jacksonville. This trip was not at all what he expected. Stephanie initiated having relations. At first, Grant wasn't with it because he couldn't see having sex with her parents' room a few doors down from them. Then he thought about earlier and how he crucified her for not doing what Ashley was willing to do, so he gave into his wife. It was very passionate, more so than it had been in a while. She didn't even think about porn scenes like she usually would. This trip put Stephanie back in the game. She is ready to let go of the porn and has vowed never to indulge in it again. She declared within herself that she is done with porn!

Chapter Eight: All Behind Us?

Stephanie stuck to her vow and stayed away from porn over the last nine months, which was easy since she had embedded the images in her brain. As she would lie with her husband, the images of the sexual content she had seen would flashback throughout her mind and build up her expectation. Mostly, her expectation was not met due to her comparing her husband to what she saw in the flicks. She didn't think this was wrong at all. It was something a little extra that heightened their sex life. She was too ashamed to get help and tell anyone about her problem, instead focused on her relationship with Grant and supporting his dreams. He finally found a manager position at a research facility. They were glad to have him because they knew of his excellent work and the success he had with the autism clinical study. He's been there for the past two months. It has drastically changed his persona because now he's working doing what he loves, has his wife with him all the time, but he does miss going to church with Stephanie. She has avoided going to church all these months, claiming she has to work even though she's the one in charge of making the schedules.

"Wake up, babe. Your alarm is going off," Grant said.

"Ugh," Stephanie said groggily.

"Get up so you can go to work," Grant said.

"I don't have to work today. I forgot to turn off my alarm," she continued to say half-sleep.

"Oh, you don't," he said.

"No, now let me go back to sleep. I'm exhausted," she said.

"Well, since you don't have to work today, you can go to church with me this morning."

Stephanie's eyes bucked open, and she popped up and said, "Today is Sunday?"

"Yep. No more excuses."

"Awh man!"

"What are you awh manning about? You should be happy now that we finally get a chance to go to church together."

"I don't want to go, Grant."

"Why not?"

"I'm just tired. I've been working double shifts all week."

"But it's been over a year since we've been at church together. I miss that Steph."

"I know, but you know I've been working on Sundays. It's not my fault."

"Yes, it is."

"What do you mean?"

"Steph, I don't know how slow you think I am, but even I know that you are the one that makes the schedules."

She looked surprised and replied, "How do you know that?"

"If you are in charge of the kitchen, that means everything, right? That's what you told me, right?"

"Look, Grant, I'm tired, and I'm not going. Period! Now stop pestering me."

"Oh, I'm pestering you? You haven't seen anything yet!"

He picks up the phone, and Stephanie asked, "What are you doing?"

"I'm calling your mama."

"You better put down that phone!" She waited for a few seconds and continued, "I'm not playing!"

"Hey, mom. How are you doing?" Grant asked.

On the other end of the telephone conversation, Stephanie can't hear what's going on and becomes agitated as she listens to what she can hear, and that's Grant spilling the beans. "Mom, you know how you and dad have been asking how's church? Well, I haven't been all that truthful with you. Steph has not been going to church since we've been here."

Then Stephanie heard a loud, "What!" from the other end of the phone. She let out a little giggle, though, because her mom sounded like that one mom on the Christmas Story movie. Grant continued, "I didn't know how to tell you guys. I've been going, but she won't go with me. I have been patient, but now it has become tiring. She won't go with me this morning even though she doesn't have to work. This is her first Sunday that she hasn't "scheduled" herself in months."

Stephanie knew what was coming next because there was a long pause on Grant's end, then he said, "Hold on," with a smirk on his face, and handed Stephanie the telephone. She hesitated for a couple of seconds, took a deep breath, and said, "Hey mama!" in a voice of excitement as if she had no clue of what's going on.

"Don't hey me. What is this nonsense about you not going to church?"

"Mama, Grant is just making this out to be a bigger deal than what it really is. I have worked all week, and this is my only day off, and I would like to rest."

"Are you choosing to work all week?" Mrs. Chase asked.

"I have no choice but to pull up the slack when employees don't do their job and show up to work."

"I don't care for your tone."

"I'm sorry, mama."

"There is more that you're not telling me. It's not like you to skip out on church. Now, what's really going on?"

"Nothing, mama. I'm just tired."

"You know I'm going to find out, don't you?"

"You always do, but I'm telling you there is nothing else to it."

"Go to church with your husband today."

"But mama…"

"Don't make me come to Jacksonville. You know, I will." Mrs. Chase said in her firm, don't mess with me voice.

"Yes, mama."

"Let me speak back to my son-in-law."

"She wants to speak back to you," Stephanie said as she handed Grant back the telephone.

"Yes, ma'am?" Grant said, speaking with Mrs. Chase.

Stephanie knew her mother was giving Grant the business because all she heard was, "Yes, ma'am. Yes ma'am. Yes ma'am, a long pause then more yes ma'ams to follow. She went to get a shower but was madder than a cat in water. She could have lit Grant ablaze. Stephanie was going to make sure Grant regretted what he just did.

The drive on the way to the place of worship was quieter than church folk's response when it's time to tithe. He was trying to hold conversations with Stephanie while they were in the car, but she gave him not even a hum for a response. He got the picture that he was in hot water, but it didn't fade him. Grant figured it would be rough getting her to go, and he was willing to endure it. He cares about his wife's soul more than her childish antics. They parked and went inside the church. Stephanie thought she was going to go up in flames as she entered. All she could think about was what she was doing just nine months ago. How could she be accepted? Would these same folks be as welcoming if they knew what she had done? Moreover, would her own parents? She stayed quiet as they walked through the foyer into the sanctuary. Grant introduced her to his fellow brothers and sisters in Christ. Some of the females gave her dirty looks. They would have just liked for him to keep coming by himself.

Pastor Sims brought forth a mighty word and it kind of reminded Stephanie of back home. She could see why Grant liked it so much and why he wanted her to come. During the message, Grant slowly reached to hold her hand, and she let go of her anger and let him.

Once church was over, Grant took Stephanie towards the Pastor's office to introduce her to the pastor and his wife. Co-Pastor Sims hugged her and said, "It's so good to finally meet you! Grant talks about you often. Your husband sure does love you."

"I know," Stephanie said with a smile looking at Grant.

"He's a good man. I want him to become a part of my staff, but he wants to wait for you to join the church with him," said Pastor Sims.

"I know that he would be honored to be on your staff. He doesn't have to wait on me, though. My schedule is pretty tight at work, and I don't want to join if I can't commit to something. He has my full support." She knew exactly how to respond in her experienced "church" way.

"Sir, I hear what she says, but I still want to wait for her," Grant said.

"I understand, son," said Pastor Sims, patting him on his shoulder.

"Well, it was nice meeting you guys," Stephanie said, signifying it's time to go.

Pastor Sims and his wife simultaneously responded with, "It was nice meeting you too." Grant and Stephanie left and headed home.

"Steph, do you want to go out to eat before heading home?" asked Grant.

"Sure. What did you have in mind?"

"A buffet, maybe?"

"No, I'm not in the mood for a buffet."

"What are you in the mood for?"

"Can we just pick up something and take it home?"

"Are you alright?"

"Yes, I just want to go home and relax. I'm up on my feet and going for hours on end all week long, and I just want to rest."

"Well, I will take you home and go get us something to eat. That way, you can get a shower, relax, and kick your feet up."

"That's a plan I can get with."

Grant did just what he said he was going to do. Stephanie took off her church clothes and kicked her feet up, watching television. As she flipped through the cable network, she ran across the adult channels. She paused and thought back on the day's event; how all church did was remind her of her sin. When she pressed select on one of the adult movies, all it did was remind her of what her sin took from her. She felt trapped. There was nowhere to go and nothing she felt like she could do about it. The sin confined her to an invisible jail, but she didn't realize that no one had the key to release her except her. She turned off her television, did something else with her time, and decided not to watch TV until Grant returned home. She was committed to being done with porn.

While at home, she decided to develop some new recipes that she could introduce as a special dish at the restaurant. Stephanie has high hopes of opening her own restaurant one day, which would be a great way to see if people would like her food. She picked up a pen and paper and began to accumulate ideas, putting a twist on America's favorite foods.

It wasn't before long that Grant came through the door to find his wife working. She was into it too.

"What are you doing? I thought you wanted to rest," Grant asked.

"Yes, I did, but some ideas for recipes were flying through my head, so I had to write them down," she answered.

"Well, here is your food," he said.

"You're going to eat with me, aren't you?"

"I thought you were working, so I didn't want to bother you."

"Awh, you're jealous. That's so cute."

"Man, I ain't cute. That's for stuffed animals."

"Relax, Grant, I was just doing this until you returned home. I was bored. I guess I can't sit around."

"What do you want to watch?"

"Can we just eat and talk to each other?"

"Of course."

They began eating their lunch and talking. Stephanie asked him about his experiments and clinical study at work, and his eyes lit up with excitement. She really could have cared less because all of it was foreign to her, but to see her husband's face light up when talking about doing what he loves, she respected it. Then he started down a path that she could have never talked about ever.

"So, what did you think about church today?"

"It was good. I can see how you would go there."

"What was good about it?"

"It reminded me of back home. I miss home."

"Me too, but Jacksonville will work for a while."

"Yeah, I guess. I really miss my parents. Even though we've been here for some time now, I can't get over not seeing my parents every day. I've never been away from them like this, and things probably would have been different if I hadn't moved away."

"Maybe it's not as bad as it seems. You have to get used to the idea of being out on your own and growing up into a mature adult."

"Yeah, I know, but..."

"But what?"

"I don't know; maybe I'm overthinking it."

"You'll work through it."

"I guess I will have no choice but to work it out."

After a long pause in their conversation, Grant asked Stephanie, "Will you go back to church with me?"

"As long as the schedule permits," Stephanie answered with no intention of returning.

"Can you work the schedule to make it more often?" Grant said with a glimmer of hope.

"I will try."

"You promise?"

"Yes, I promise," Stephanie said, knowing it was a lie when she said it, but she didn't want to ruin the moment.

Chapter Nine: Failed Perfection

"Steph, what's wrong?" Grant asked, a little irritated with her as he stopped in the middle of sex because he could tell his wife wasn't into it at all.

"Nothing Grant. Keep going," she said.

"I'm not in the mood."

"Why? What happened?"

"You!"

"Me, what did I do?"

"You're not as passionate as you usually are. This has been going on for a while now, and I'm fed up."

"I don't understand."

"You say you don't, but you do."

"But I don't know where all this is coming from."

"You play these games, and I thought we were past this. Women throw themselves at me all the time, but I ignore it because of you but Stephanie, you give me nothing in return, nothing to stay. You work all the time, don't go to church, inactive in bed, and barely do any housework. I mean, if I'm doing everything, I should live by myself."

"Tell me how you really feel."

"This ain't a joke!"

"And I ain't laughing."

"Steph, you've changed. You're not the woman I fell in love with."

"What happened to the take-charge man I fell in love with? Do you think I don't have qualms? I mean, for real, I would never say things to you that you just said to me. I wouldn't hurt you that way, but I guess you don't care. If I'm really that bad and you want to be on your own, then do what you gotta do. I can't keep you here if you don't want to stay. I am not in the keepsake business."

"Steph…," Grant said in a softer tone as he grabbed her arm to keep her from walking out of the room.

"Let go of me," she said as she jerked her arm away. She got dressed and left the house.

Stephanie couldn't wait to get to her car, so she could actually do what's in her heart to do, and that was to cry. Running down the stairs to beat the tears that were about to fall down her face, she could hear Grant yelling for her to come back. The neighbor across the hall heard the ruckus and went to see what was going on, and she saw Grant with his shirt off and baggy jeans low over his hips. She could tell he didn't have on anything underneath the jeans. The neighbor looked at him, smiled, and winked at him while opening her door wider, gesturing for him to come inside. Grant looked at the lady who appeared to be and was every bit of seventy years old; his body shuttered at the thought and closed the door.

By this time, Stephanie made it to her car, but her tears beat her there; however, the rain hid them. Her eyes welled up by water so heavy she couldn't pull out of the parking space. Grant looked out the window and saw her sitting there. He felt like the worst person in the world for the things he said to his wife. It was how he felt, but he could have sat down with her and shared his concerns in a better way. The rain started to pour. He hesitated, but after a few minutes went by, he noticed she was still there, so he put on a shirt just in case the neighbor came back out and went to talk to his wife. Stephanie was weeping with her head laid on the steering wheel.

"Steph!" Grant said as he knocked on the window. She heard him but didn't move. He gave her a chance to open the door on her own, but since she didn't, he unlocked the door with his keys. She wouldn't look up at him nor respond to him in any way. "Stephanie, come on upstairs with me, please. I'm sorry, Steph." She still didn't respond. He slid her out of the car, picked her up, and carried her back to the apartment. She couldn't stop crying. It was for more reasons other than what Grant said to her. She couldn't believe this was happening. She knew where she went wrong. Grant carried her through the door, sat down on the couch with her on his lap. She hid her face in his chest, and he wiped her face with his shirt and moved her wet hair out of her eyes. It crushed him to think of how he hurt her so bad.

"Stephanie, baby, I'm so sorry. I shouldn't have said those things to you."

"Do you really want to go," she managed to muffle out.

"You know I don't. Steph, you are my life. There isn't another woman for me."

"Then why would you bring up other women?"

"I was mad, but I still shouldn't have said that to you."

"I'm sorry. I've just been so exhausted from work. I don't mean to make you feel as though I'm not pleased."

"I love you, Steph," Grant said as he kissed her on her forehead.

"I love you too," Stephanie said in return. She continued, "Did that old lady across the hall say what I think she said when I was leaving?"

Grant laughed, "She invited me to her house."

"Eww, that's just nasty."

They laughed, and Grant stared into his wife's eyes, and he could still see the hurt. He gently gave her a kiss on her forehead, then whispered in her ear, "You are my life, Stephanie. She kissed him on the lips. Stephanie gave in, and making up from the argument gave her the passion she needed that Grant was looking for all along. However, she also knew what she had to do to keep him happy. It's the only way. When he picked up his wife to take her to the bedroom, she said, "I'm going to have to mark you up to let these chicks know about me," and started kissing him on his neck. He laid her down on the bed and said, "You need not worry. They already know about you." If Grant was a singer on stage, Stephanie would have thrown her panties at him after saying something like that. He was skilled in the game and knew just what to say!

The next day, Stephanie called into work. She made sure her staff was well advised and in place because she wouldn't be back into work for a few days. She wanted to make sure things were right with her husband. Grant took off work too but could only do it for one day. They drove to Daytona Beach and explored the city, and spent the day there. They had a great time. It felt good to get away for a while. It was like one of their dates when they were dating. They took goofy pictures in the picture booth, went to the mall, and did some shopping. They went to a restaurant and had a Grade A dinner, then walked on the beach. It got late, and Grant realized that he wouldn't be on time for work the next day. He made a few phone calls to let his supervisor know he'd be late. They stayed overnight but left before the sun came up the next morning. Grant and Stephanie hadn't laughed and had fun like that in so long it almost felt strange. From the outside looking in, one would never know the drama they went through the night before.

When they arrived home the next day, Stephanie dropped Grant off at work and headed home. She cleaned the house from top to bottom, cooked dinner, then sat down and watched television until Grant came home from work.

Stephanie received an alert on her phone, letting her know that she received an email. She opened it, and it was one of the porn sites she subscribed to a while ago. The emails had been coming for months, but she always deleted them, but she decided to open them this time. She didn't want Grant feeling the way he felt just a couple of nights ago. The images she depended on some time ago began to fade. When it came to sex with her husband, Stephanie didn't have anything to get her juices flowing. It had nothing to do with Grant but all to do with how porn programmed her mind.

Porn addiction is just like being addicted to crack, heroin, and weed; it makes you believe you need that high, and that is what Stephanie is going through. She went without watching porn for too long, and her body no longer knows how to respond. It only responded to the stimulation of porn. The brain sent messages to her body about what she needed, and she didn't know what to do about it. She definitely couldn't talk to him about it and especially not her parents. This was a battle she had to take on all by herself. The shame that came with this sin was greater than drugs and alcoholism. People expect that kind of addiction, but this is a sexual sin, and folks act crazy when it comes to this kind of sin. They lock away their husbands and boyfriends as if you want them, and it's nothing like that, or they spread lies and rumors about you, or they talk about you like a dog with no owner.

Taking a chance opening that email, Stephanie didn't realize what was happening; she was engulfed in the porn. Three hours had passed since the email alert. That's what happens with porn; what seems like only moments in time are actually great lengths of times within the moments. The only way she knew so much time passed was because she heard Grant's voice talking to someone in the hallway. She got off her phone and turned to a channel he wouldn't question her watching. Grant's keys were in the door, and the lock was turning. She ended up playing one of the shows she recorded on DVR. She cleared the history on her phone. She usually watches it on a private browser. Even if he went through her phone, nothing watched from the private browser would show up because it's automatically deleted. Grant walked through the door, smelled the freshness of a clean home and a cooked meal. He looked at his wife, and a huge smile came across his face.

"Hey, how was work?" Stephanie asked as she got up off the couch to give him a kiss hello.

"I missed you all day, so that's how my day went," Grant said, kissing her on the forehead.

"Awh, isn't that sweet. I got you whipped like that?"

"Me? Whipped? I don't know about all that."

"It's alright. You don't have to admit it. I see it all over your face."

"Girl, you crazy."

"I gotta be me."

"Home looks great. What you cook for dinner?"

"Orange chicken, fried rice, and some egg rolls."

"Shoot, I'm ready. Let's eat."

"Sit down and watch TV. I'll bring you a plate. What do you want to drink?"

"Some ice-cold water."

"Water it is."

She fixed their plates. They ate and chilled watching TV. He had no question about what she had done that day because it was evident. There was nothing that indicated otherwise, nor did his mind go to her watching porn. They enjoyed their time together and had a blessed night.

Chapter Ten: Busted!

Over the next few days, Stephanie repeated the same process while off work. She loved that her husband was happy. They hadn't argued or fussed or even had a small disagreement. This is the kind of life they were both meant to have, and this is what she continued to desire. Stephanie eventually went back to work but kept up with what she had to do at home to keep her husband happy, although it was exhausting. He helped too. He refused to allow her to do all the work. They switched cooking dinner and cleaning up the house. Grant still had to beg her to go to church with him, though, because she wasn't budging. He called in the big guns.

It was a Saturday night, and Stephanie had a rough day at work. All she wanted to do was to go home and fall asleep in her husband's arms. She figured since the day had exhausted itself, nothing else could go wrong. She drove out of her restaurant's parking lot at 11:30 pm and pulled up to her apartment complex at 11:53 pm. She was depleted of any energy she had left as she used every bit of the last drop to walk upstairs to enter her home. Stephanie walked through the door and stumbled through the dark house. She went to her bedroom, got a shower, and plopped in the bed. Grant rolled over and gave her a kiss on her forehead and said, "I love you." She responded in kind and went to sleep.

Sunday morning, the alarm went off as it usually does for Grant to get up and get ready for church. He tried waking Stephanie up, but she wouldn't budge. She grudgingly mumbled some words saying she wasn't going. Grant didn't worry about it and continued to get himself ready. He stepped out of their bedroom and left Stephanie to herself. She noticed he didn't make a big fuss this time and murmured, "Thank you, Jesus. Won't He do it," and pulled the covers over her head and fell back to sleep.

"Stephanie, it's time to get up for church," a familiar voice said. Stephanie shook her head in ignorance as if she was hearing something and closed her eyes. Then a few minutes later, she heard it again, "Stephanie, get up, and I'm not going to tell you again." By this time, she was ticked off because Grant went too far. She was going to check him and kindly go right back to sleep. At the same time, she pulled the covers off her and tried to sit up in the bed; she said, "Grant, I don't…"

"I am not Grant. Now get up right now," the familiar voice said.

"Daddy? What are you doing here?" Stephanie asked.

"Getting you all the way together. We'll talk later, but right now, you need to get up and get ready for church because you're making us late," Mr. Chase said.

"Yes, sir," Stephanie replied. She got a glimpse of Grant standing behind Mr. Chase with a smirk on his face. No wonder he wasn't pushy this morning. Stephanie wanted to wring his neck. "Excuse me, sir," Grant said, getting by his father-in-law to make up the bed. He was smiling the whole time too. Stephanie waited until her father stepped outside their room, so she could get ready, and as soon as he did, she went in on Grant, saying in a whispered manner, "How could you do this? You told on me? That's childish!"

Loudly, Grant responded, "Stop yelling at me."

Stephanie whispered again, "Are you serious right now? This is how you want to do this?"

"Steph, no! Stop!" Grant yelled, still making up the bed.

There was a knock on their bedroom door, and Mr. Chase said, "Leave him alone and get ready. Don't have me come in there."

"But daddy," she whined.

"But nothing. You heard what I said," Mr. Chase said.

Stephanie did not go back and forth with her father. She knew brotha man didn't play that. He was old school, and she was not going to gamble at ruffling those feathers. She stormed off and stomped her way to the bathroom giving Grant the silent treatment. He didn't care. He wanted her in church. It was important to him. For goodness sake, she was the reason he gave his life to Christ, but he soon realized that her being the reason wasn't enough to keep him in a relationship with God. He had to want Him for himself. Grant took his relationship with God deeper, and while he swam deeper in God, he wanted Stephanie to come along.

On their way to church, Mr. Chase fussed the whole way. She sat in the backseat with him while her mother sat in the front with Grant. They were getting a kick out of it, although Mrs. Chase was a little disappointed in her daughter. She never thought Stephanie would have turned her back on God. She loved Him, always have, ever since she was a little girl. Stephanie was the first one up, always singing and participating in ministry, sitting and talking with the elderly, helping those in need without being told, and everyone loved her. Mrs. Chase couldn't figure out what went wrong, but Mr. Chase was sure to get to the bottom of it. Stephanie was in the backseat hotter than a jalapeno being charred on a gas stove. They pulled up to the church and walked inside. Grant tried to hold Stephanie's hand, but she wasn't having it. Mr. Chase saw what she was doing, and he pinched the back of her arm ever so slightly, just like when she was a kid. "Ouch, Daddy," she belted. "Then get yourself together," Mr. Chase whispered, grinding his teeth. She held Grant's hand grudgingly while tears weld up in her eyes. His pinches hurt, and it took her back to when she was a little girl. It put her in her place, though. She didn't give Grant any more problems after that…or just until after they left. Stephanie played the game. She played the good, lovey-dovey wife. I mean, it was a spectacle. Mr. and Mrs. Chase had never seen their daughter act so defiant before. She didn't get into trouble much when she was a child. They would correct her, and she'd straighten right up. She was never the problem child. The preacher preached, but Stephanie didn't hear a word of it. They may have made her go, but that doesn't mean she had to listen. She thought of everything else other than giving that preacher the time of day.

After service, Grant introduced his in-laws to the pastor and his wife. They had a long conversation. Stephanie was tired of waiting, so she excused herself, pretending she had to go to the restroom and instead headed straight out the church doors. She went and sat in the car while they talked. She turned on the AC and some music and went to sleep. She made it seem like they were taking forever, but it was only for about fifteen minutes. Eventually, after she'd been asleep for a few minutes, they walked out of the church laughing and talking. They got into the car, and she pretended to still be asleep. They ignored her and went on about their conversation. They grabbed something to eat at a buffet-style restaurant. Mrs. Chase stared at her daughter the whole time. While the men grabbed them something to eat, Mrs. Chase saw her window of opportunity to open dialogue and said, "Okay, Stephanie, what's really going on with you?"

"Nothing, momma," Stephanie replied, a little annoyed.

"Something is going on, but you're keeping it bottled up. Why?"

"There's nothing wrong, mama."

"This is not. You're not my daughter. My daughter wouldn't behave like this."

"Your daughter has different challenges now, so no, I'm not the same person."

"Tell me what it is, and maybe I can help."

"There's nothing you can do. I'm working on it myself."

"What has happened, Stephanie? You barely call us anymore; you won't go to church; we used to be able to talk about anything and everything."

"Mama, Grant was wrong for calling y'all."

"No, he was right. He's just as concerned about you as we are. We hear from him more than we hear from you. Did you know they want to elevate him at church?"

"To what?"

"That's something Grant should tell you, but you are the hold-up. He won't do it without you."

"That's not my fault."

"Okay, keep up with these smart-ellic answers, and you are going to find yourself alone."

"Alone? What are you talking about?"

"You don't think those women in that church notice he comes through the doors by himself. Oh, baby, they notice. I'd suggest you protect your "investment" if you're still in favor of the "stock.""

"I know about them, hot-tailed women. I ain't worried."

"And I'm not saying you should be, but what I am saying, your presence needs to be made known. It's about being a praying woman, and you ain't praying, baby. You're leaving your husband, your marriage, and your home open to the enemy, and he's tearing it up. How do you know what to pray if you're not around? This restaurant you work at can't be a good fit for you because nothing that is of God will rip to shreds what He took time to build. All I'm asking you to do is to start praying again."

"I pray, mama."

"No, you don't because if you did, we wouldn't be here, nor would we be having this conversation."

"I'm good, mama."

"Okay, but whenever you are ready to talk to me, I'm here." Mrs. Chase said as she got up to grab her some food. She was really concerned about her daughter and knew there was more going on than she was saying. The fellas came back to the table, and Stephanie left to get her some food. She was tired of everyone getting on her and didn't want to have any more conversations. She stayed quiet most of the time and was very short answered when she spoke, and Grant was displeased.

Shortly after, Stephanie's parents left to return home. They stayed a week to see if there was anything they could see spiritually. Nothing came to them except she seemed to spend a lot of time alone, secluded, and on her phone. Stephanie tried to be discreet about it, but it showed. They prayed for their daughter and made a vow to call once a week to check on her. Grant is good about contacting them and chatting. He talks to them more than his own parents.

Stephanie wanted Grant to pay for what he did, so she held out for a whole month. He would make advances, and she would turn him down flat. She was getting hers through what her eyes viewed, and her body responded in pleasure, so she could have cared less if he was getting his or not. He would think twice about calling her parents and telling on her again. "By the time he gets a piece of this again, he will be grateful," she thought to herself. Little did she know that Grant was hesitating and contemplating about calling Ashley again. Ashely had been calling since his last visit. He doesn't see the plot she has in place. He gave up someone who really wanted to be with him for someone who's playing games. Grant picked up the phone to call her a few times but wavered whether he should or shouldn't. He got away scot-free the first time and the second time and wasn't sure that would happen again. He didn't want to frustrate the grace of God, plus he loved God and didn't want to do anything to hurt his relationship with Him. He reasoned within himself he's probably going through this because of the affair he hasn't fessed up to yet. He decided to tell Stephanie when she gets home from work. He was scared and didn't know how she was going to take it. He prayed and prayed and prayed some more for God to lead him in how to tell her.

Hours later, Stephanie arrived home. She was in an alright mood, which was a good thing. She walked right past Grant, still being mad at him. "Hey Steph, how was work?" he asked.

"It was good. Just a regular day," she answered.

"Go ahead and get your shower, and I will bring dinner to you."

"Thank you." She went into her room and locked the door. She got a shower and unlocked the door, so Grant could bring in her dinner, but she received a message on her phone when she stepped out. She checked it and sat down on her bed. Quickly she became engaged in the video that played on her phone, forgetting she unlocked the door. Grant walked in, and she jumped. Then said, "Whew, you scared me," as she cleverly pressed the close button on her phone. "Here's your plate," Grant said. Stephanie got up, put on some pajamas, and then sat right back on the bed with her phone near her side. She ate her food and wished for Grant to leave the room to finish watching her video. Grant took a deep breath and said, "Hey Steph, I have something really important I need to tell you." She knew if she stayed short answered with him, he'd leave the room, and it played out just that way. "Yeah, what's up?" she said as she viewed pictures on her social media, completely ignoring her husband. "Can you put your phone down for at least a few minutes? You might want to hear this," he said. "Naw, I'm good," she nonchalantly answered. "But Steph…," he began to say. "I'm listening. Go ahead and say what you gotta say," she said rudely and still on her phone. "Forget it!" Grant said and walked out of the room, slamming the door. As soon as he left the room, she went right back to watching her video and said, "About time." Grant, hearing what she said, blasted back through the door. She couldn't close out the video fast enough before Grant snatched her phone out of her hands. When he saw what she was watching, the moment seemed like it stood still. He was speechless. Here it is he was about to spill his guts, and his wife is being turned on by watching other people having sex. He came to the fact; he wasn't the problem, and he wasn't going to tell her a thing. Then it was like they were snatched out of the frozen moment and reality rushed back through them instantly. Grant said disheartened, "I'm done. Stephanie, I can't compete with this," as he threw her phone on the bed beside her. Stephanie rushed to his side and said, "Grant, I'm sorry." He snatched his arm back from her hold, saying nothing. He collected his keys and some clothes. Stephanie was sobbing in apologies and pleading for him to stay. He walked out, saying nothing to his wife. Grant had no idea where he would go, but he knew he had to get out of there. He needed to talk to somebody and quick. He'd grown close to some of the men at church but was too embarrassed about what was going on in his own house. What would that say about his manhood? He decided to go to a hotel and be by himself. He didn't want a marriage like his parents, and that's what this seemed to be turning into.

Stephanie couldn't stop crying. She tried calling him, but it just went to voicemail. He got tired of her calling, so he turned his phone off. There seemed to be no words that could heal the open scar on his soul or soothe the massive hit his ego just took.

Ashley plotted and planned for the perfect time to make her move. Grant didn't know, but she had the location app on her phone. Ashley was able to pinpoint where Grant was, and she saw he was at a hotel. She made that drive. She didn't care if Stephanie was there or not; she was going to put her plans into motion.

When she arrived at the hotel, she knocked on the door. Grant didn't know who it was because no one knew he was there. He opened the door with caution.

"Hello, sailor," Ashley said when Grant opened the door.

"How'd you know I was here?"

"Don't worry about that. Aren't you going to let me in?" Grant opened the door all the way and gestured for her to enter.

"Nobody knows I'm here, so how did you know?" Grant asked and he ain't in the mood for her shenanigans.

"Why is that important? I'm here now."

"I ain't for your BS right now. Did you go to my place? Did you tell Stephanie?"

"Why are you worried about her? Cause it seems like she's not taking care of you; otherwise, you wouldn't be here."

"I ain't got time for this. There's something not right about you being here. The fact you knew I was here, and nobody else didn't don't sit straight with me."

"Don't be like that. Let me take care of you," Ashley said stroking his chest.

"No, I think it's time for you to go," Grant said.

Ashley opened her coat seductively and said, "Are you sure?"

Grant glanced upon this gorgeous body that was only 5% dressed and said, "You came here like that?"

"You miss this, don't you?"

"You have no idea," Grant said as he picked her up and laid her on the bed. His soul was conflicted. He felt free with this woman with absolutely no responsibilities, no ties, no bondage. All Ashley wanted was to be with him. He really didn't care for her like he did Stephanie. Ashley was for him what porn was for Stephanie, a scapegoat, a release. She was easy, not in the sexual sense but in the sense of no struggles. He classified Ashley like the women he was with before Stephanie. He knew he just told Stephanie he was done, but he really didn't feel that way. Grant knew in his heart that he wanted to be with his wife. He's just mad at her right now. While he was kissing Ashley about to proceed in the festivities, his thoughts lingered. If he went through with this, his marriage is definitely over.

Grant got up and told Ashley, "We really need to talk."

"I don't want to talk."

"You don't have a choice."

"What is so important?"

"Let me ask you a question. Why do you keep pursuing me when I've already told you I'm not leaving my wife for you?"

"That's what you say with your mouth, but your body says different. Your body tells me that you want to be with me."

"My body's reaction to you is flesh and don't mean nothing. What's in my heart is what should concern you because that's what has meaning. Why can't you understand that I love my wife?"

"If you really love her, then why am I always on your mind?"

"It's not that you are on my mind. You are what I don't have to face and deal with every day. You're my scapegoat."

"Scapegoat? That's not what you were saying when you lived in Savannah."

"I know, and I never should have knocked on your door for coffee that night. We never should have had dinner."

"But we did, and now we're here."

"Ashley, I want to apologize. I'm not the man you need. My heart belongs to Stephanie. Even though we're in a rough patch, she's my everything. I involved you in our mess, and that's not right. You never should be second best to anyone. Find you someone that loves you like I love my wife. Give me your phone."

"Why?"

"Just give it to me." She gave him her phone and deleted his number and all the texts between them she had saved. He showed her his phone while he deleted her number and texts.

"This is really over."

"Yes, Ashley, it is."

"But I love you, Grant."

"No, you don't. You love the idea of me. And I don't love you. Never have."

Grant's words crushed Ashley. He was straightforward with her, and she left the hotel, never bothering Grant again. He washed her off him, laid in the bed, and went to sleep.

Throughout the night, after endless failed phone calls, Stephanie does what she does best in tense and stressful situations, and that is to turn to her phone, laptop, and tablet. She had porn going on all three. She watched it over and over again. It didn't even make her feel better. It just took her mind off things. She fell asleep in the wee hours of the morning, completely missing work. Her phone died so no one could reach her. Grant woke up the next day and took off work. He couldn't go in this shape. He had to talk with his wife and get his mind straight. He figured she'd be at work, so he went there since he couldn't reach her on the phone. Her employees told him that she didn't show up, and they tried to call her, but it kept going to her voicemail.

Immediately, Grant was concerned and went home. He walked into their bedroom to find her laid out in the middle of the bed, surrounded by her phone, laptop, and tablet. When he scaled his finger across the screen, he saw what she'd been watching. At this point, he understood his wife had a problem, and he was going to help her through it. He didn't want to embarrass her, so he logged out of everything, closed it up, and charged her phone. He put covers over her and left out of the room. He went into the kitchen and called her job to let them know that she's okay and is at home now and she won't be at work for a week because she has to go home to handle a family emergency. Then he called her parents to get advice on what to do because he didn't know how to handle something like this. He prepared for them to head back home for the week. They hadn't been in Georgia for a long time, but it was time to go back. While she continued to sleep, Grant packed their clothes and prayed. He couldn't understand how his wife got wrapped up in this and wondered how long she was in it. Stephanie was a good girl and never engaged in things like this. It was time to put ministry in place within his own home and allow for grace to be his cushion. His wife needs grace, and outside of God, it would have to come from him as well.

Chapter Eleven: The Truth is Revealed

It was ninety-seven degrees outside, and Stephanie was wrapped up in a gray hoodie walking through the convenience store with shades on in embarrassment. Everyone gazed upon her as if she was crazy, then looked at Grant like, "You gone do something about that?" but he strove on in strength. It didn't matter how much she tried to hide her face; there was nothing she could wear that would hide the shame.

Grant didn't know how to comfort his wife; all he could do was love her. It was the hardest thing he ever had to do. Grant, himself, wasn't the most forgiving person. It kind of shocked him that he was so tolerant. He hadn't even fully forgiven his parents.

They arrived in Georgia and headed to the hotel. The only way Grant could get her to go home to Georgia was to agree to get a hotel room. She couldn't face her parents. She did not want to see them at all. They went to the hotel room and freshened up. They barely said anything to each other. There was such a loud cry in the quietness of the room. Grant wanted to say something to his wife, but no words would form. After being in the room with her for an hour and no conversation, he said, "I'll be back." Her response…, "Okay." He was getting mad, feeling confused, and his manhood was under attack. She was ashamed, feeling alone, and robbed of love from her husband, which is ironic because she robbed him of that same love. She decided to call her best friend, who seemed to be the cause of all this mess. She was the root problem. If it weren't for her "suggestion," she wouldn't be in this predicament.

"Hey, Stephanie! Long time no hear from. Girl, where you been?" Arielya asked.

"Hey, Arielya. I've been working a lot. My position demands a great deal of my time," said Stephanie.

"Well, what's been up?" asked Arielya.

"I can't even tell you where to begin," answered Stephanie.

"Do tell," said Arielya.

"In due time. What's been going on here?"

"Oh, wait a minute, you're in town?"

"Yep."

"Oh see now, we have got to get together."

"Where do you want to go?"

"Let's go to our favorite place like we used to do as kids."

"Are you serious?"

"Yeah! It will be fun."

"So, you want to go to the church playground?"

"Yep."

"Alright then, let's go, but you are going to have to come and get me. I don't have a car."

"You know that ain't a problem. I'm on my way."

Arielya picked up Stephanie, and they went to their favorite place as kids. Even when they were teenagers, they would go from time to time and have the best fun together. When Arielya and Stephanie saw each other, they screamed in excitement, played on the swings, and even ran around playing tag. "You're it," said Arielya. Stephanie chased her around and finally caught up to her and said, "Tag…." "I can't be it. Girl, I'm tired," Arielya said as both ladies fell to the ground laughing. "We are not as young as we used to be," said Stephanie. "Hunnay, you ain't neva lied," said Arielya. "Man, I forgot how hot it still is here in September," Stephanie said. "Chile, how you forget that? Why you acting brand new? You live in Florida, and I know it's hot there," Arielya said. "Yeah, but I have been gone a while," Stephanie said. "Stop it. You have only been gone two years," said Arielya. "That's a long time," Stephanie said. "No, it ain't. Not when you've lived here your whole life," Arielya said. "Whateva," Stephanie said. They walked over to the small concrete back entrance to the church. Then Arielya asked, "I know my best friend. What's on your mind?"

"I don't even know how to tell you."

"Tell me what? Is everything good with you and Grant?"

"I can't tell right now."

"Why can't you?"

"It's complicated."

"What he do! Cause you know, I got yo' back."

"That's the thing, it wasn't him. It's me, and I don't know how he's taking it."

"What you do, Steph?"

"That's what I wanted to talk to you about."

"Me?"

"Yeah, it kind of has something to do with you."

"How? I haven't talked to you in months, and even then, you haven't said nothing to me about anything. So, how do I have anything to do with your marriage?"

"Do you remember the advice you gave me when I first got married?"

"I told you a lot of stuff, and that was a long time ago, and I'm sure all of it wasn't good."

"It's not funny, Arielya."

"A'ight. Sorry. You know I'm gone crack jokes."

"Yeah, I know but seriously. I took your advice, and now I'm in a bad spot."

"What advice was that?"

"To watch porn to help me in the bedroom."

"Oookay…so what's wrong with that?"

"It's a bigger problem than you know."

"I don't see how that is a problem. It should be a solution."

"The only thing that's absolute is the chaos it's causing."

"Sounds like you blaming me for your problems."

"Uh, yeah. If it wasn't for you, I would have never even thought about porn."

"Seems like you need to take responsibility and stop pointing the finger."

"I'm not saying it's all you. I know I screwed up, but as a best friend, you should be careful with your advice."

"As a woman who makes her own choices, you should choose what's best for you."

"I guess you're right. I just can't believe I'm the cause of our problems."

"I don't understand cause from what I hear, that is not the reason."

"What you mean?"

"Nothing."

"Spill it, Arielya."

"I ain't tryin' to hurt you like that."

"Hurt me? What are you talking about?"

"I'm sorry to tell you this, but I heard when Grant was living here while you were in Florida, he was sleeping some chick."

"Grant? Naw…I don't believe that. I mean, we been through some rough stuff, but we always managed to come out of it."

"I'm just sayin' folk talk, and they said he was bumping bellies with some chick named Ashley."

"Oh, Ashley? Girl, I know it may have looked like that, but they were just working together on a documentary. Her task was to follow him around and record him. I've even spoken to her several times. She was cool. Believe me, it was nothing like that."

"Okay, if you say so, but usually where there's smoke, there's fire."

"And sometimes the fires are started by arsonists."

"You know yo' man better than I do, but you know I wasn't going to hear something like that and not say nothin'."

"I appreciate you looking out. I know you got my back."

"Always. Now, back to your freaky-deeky self."

"Whateva Arielya. Like I was trying to say, porn has taken me to a place that I haven't been able to come out of. I'm not in church anymore and feel like as soon as I walk through them doors, I'm gone get lassoed and snatched straight to hell." Arielya busted out laughing. She laughed until she cried. She said, "Whew chile, not lassoed and snatched!"

Stephanie said, "Girl, this ain't even funny." "I'm sorry, but yeah, it is," Arielya said.

Stephanie continued, "While you laughing, I can't give myself completely to Grant because all I can see when we have sex are the images in my head.

I'm watching it all the time and use the excuse that I'm learning moves, so he would be pleased, which was why I started watching it in the beginning, but you know what, Arielya, he's not."

"Not what?"

"Pleased."

"Why you say that?"

"Because it's true."

Meanwhile, Grant got more upset at the hotel because Stephanie wasn't answering his phone calls. Stephanie's parents were waiting on them, and he couldn't reach his wife. She didn't leave a note or call to say where she was going. He called her one last time, and it went to voicemail. In turn, he called her parents and told them he couldn't reach her, so they called Arielya because that was the only other person her parents knew she would be with right now.

Arielya looked at her phone and said, "It's Mama Chase."

"Don't tell them I with you," Stephanie said.

"Hey, Mama Chase," Arielya said as she answered the phone.

"How are you doing, Arielya?" asked Mrs. Chase.

"I'm good. How have you been?" Arielya asked.

"The same," answered Mrs. Chase.

"What can I do you for?" asked Arielya.

"Girl, you are so silly," said Mrs. Chase.

"You know me, Mama Chase. I get my clown on," said Arielya. Stephanie looked at her best friend and just giggled within herself.

"Yes, I do know you, chile. Have you seen Stephanie?" asked Mrs. Chase.

"Wait…she's here? OMG! Why didn't someone tell me she was coming? I wouldn't have made plans to go out of town," said Arielya.

"So, you haven't talked to her or seen her," asked Mrs. Chase.

She paused, looked at Stephanie, who was waving her hand and shaking her head no, and responded, "No ma'am."

"Okay. Thank you, Arielya. That pause was just the answer that I needed," said Mrs. Chase.

"What you mean, Mama Chase?" Arielya asked.

"Nothing at all. Thanks," said Mrs. Chase as she hung up the phone.

"Steph, we better get out of here. I think Mama Chase knew I was lying," said Arielya.

"Who wouldn't with that big long pause you just gave. You slippin' man. You know she gone find us," Stephanie said.

"She always do," said Arielya.

"Well, we ain't going to make it easy for her. Let's dip," Stephanie said.

Arielya and Stephanie left their childhood playground and went to a small café shop in Richmond Hill, which was almost a half an hour away from where they were. They took some crazy selfies, posted them on Arielya's photo social media page, ordered their beverages, and sat down to finish talking.

"Mmm…this is really good," Stephanie said.

"I know, right. I come here all the time," said Arielya.

"I see why?"

"Enough small talk. So, tell me how I'm ruining your marriage with porn."

"I'm going to come from it from this angle since you wouldn't listen to me in the car. What happens to you when you watch porn?"

"Gurl, that's personal."

"Are you going to take this seriously or not?"

"I am serious, and that is seriously personal."

"Come on, be real with me. You always talk about keeping it 100, so keep it 100 right now."

"You make it sound like I watch it all the time. I don't watch it like that. It doesn't have that kind of hold on me."

"That wasn't my question."

"I only watch it from time to time."

"You're avoiding my question. Let me ask it this way. Why do you watch it?"

"I don't know. One day I wasn't, and the next day I was."

"Who got you started on porn?"

"I don't know. It was just a group of us. We were over LaDayia's house that day. I believe you were at a church revival, and you know your mama did not get down with LaDayia nor her parents."

"And with good reason."

"I guess…anyway…Jason brought over a tape, and we all started watching it. That's the day her and Tate got together."

"I remember you telling me about that but not about the porn."

"Yeah, girl, they were almost getting it on right in front of us, but then she put us out, and you best believe Tate didn't follow."

"They didn't last long."

"You know how she do. She hops from one bed to another and still does."

"So you're telling me that since then, porn has not had any effect on you?"

"No, it hasn't."

"So, you don't masturbate watching it or nothing?"

"I ain't said all that. I gots to know how it feels so I can tell whatever dumbfounded ninja where to go so I can get mine before he gets his."

"That's my point right there. In all the advice you gave me about porn, you didn't say that it was going to take the place of Grant."

Arielya, confused at the statement, looked at Stephanie and said, "Take the place of Grant…huh…girl…what is you talking about?"

"The only way I get turned on is by replaying the images through my mind."

"Girl, bye! All a man has to do for me is start kissing and rubbing in the right places, and I'm there. I don't know what you into?"

"I'm into watching it every day."

"Did you learn something?"

"Come on. Stop playing."

"Well, shoot, I mean, if you gone watch it every day, at least let it help you become crafty in the bedroom."

"Grant doesn't like it, or at least he claims he doesn't, but I can tell when he's enjoying it. And he says he doesn't want another woman in the bed with him; he wants me in the bed, not what I've watched."

"What? I ain't never heard that before."

"Grant is not your typical man. He's genuine right down to his very core, and if he wants something a certain way, he gets it."

"Sounds a little selfish to me."

"Really? That sounds selfish."

"I mean, yeah. What about you and what you want?"

"But can you actually say this is healthy for me and our relationship?"

"Look, I ain't tell you to watch that joint every day. I just told you to learn some things. Sounds like there's a little freak in you."

"You just gone keep cuttin' up, huh?"

"I'm just sayin'."

"Anyway, Arielya, I'm in real trouble here. How am I supposed to face my parents?"

"Why would you have to face them?"

"Cause Grant called them and told them what is going on."

"Wait a minute…Grant knows, and he snitched? Dawg, he don't know snitches get stitches?"

"Yeah, he knows. And he a snitch all day long. This ain't his first time telling on me."

"I didn't think he knew anything, but you gone have to do something about all that snitching."

"Yeah, I got to get that snitch under control. At first, he didn't know, but after confronting me a few times, I guess he noticed."

"You guess?"

"I don't know how he found out, to be honest, but either way, he's fed up and walked out."

"He walked out on you?"

"Yes, and I pretty much told him to, but he came back. Now, he's told them, but the only way I would agree to come was to stay in a hotel. I can't stay with them to see the look of disappointment on their faces."

"I don't know what to say. I'm sorry. I didn't know it was going to take a toll on you like that. It just doesn't affect me that way."

"I don't know how I got engulfed in this. I'm not this type of person. I feel like some type of drug addict."

"Well, then it's time to get you some help," Arielya said as she gestured for her BFFL to head to the car.

Arielya took Stephanie back to the hotel, feeling bad about what she led her friend into, and hoped she would get the help she needed. Stephanie sat at the restaurant bar before heading upstairs to what she knew would be a fight. She ignored her husband's calls and had Arielya lying to her mother; this addiction was sure to send her further down a rabbit hole.

After waiting an hour and a half, she headed up to her room, took a deep breath, and opened the door. When she walked in, there was no sign of Grant in which; she gave a sigh of relief but quickly gasped at the familiar face that was staring back at her.

"Daddy!" Stephanie said in shock. "What are you doing here?" she asked.

"We need to talk," Mr. Chase said.

"I know, daddy. I know," she said.

"Come here, Pumpkin," Mr. Chase said as he called her the nickname he would use to comfort her as a child. He patted the chair next to him for her to sit down. Reluctantly, she sat down, and he looked at his daughter and said, "I love you, Stephanie."

"I love you too, daddy."

"You know…you and your brothers and sister didn't see your mother, and I argue a lot when you were young."

"No, we didn't."

"And we wanted it that way, but your mother and I struggled for a long time, many years."

"We didn't know that."

"You weren't supposed to because we had no plans on giving up on our marriage but to get through it. When we first started out, it was great. We didn't have problems for many years. But there came a time when I went outside our marriage."

"Daddy, you had an affair?"

"Yes, I did, but not in the conventional sense."

"What does that mean?"

"I stepped out of our marriage through porn."

Taken back at what her father just admitted to her, she said, "Through porn? That's not an affair? That doesn't make sense."

"Yes, it is. I may not have literally slept with another woman. Still, I put other women that I was watching before your mother. I compared her to them, and when she couldn't live up to what I was watching the other women do on the tapes, I ridiculed her and left unsatisfied."

"This TMI…TMI…too much information. I don't need to hear this from you. It's awkward."

"Sit back down, Stephanie, and hear what I have to say." She rolled her eyes and sat down anyway because one thing her father didn't play about was disrespect. "Look, Stephanie, I'm trying to help you save your marriage because you are the one messing it up. Do you think I ever wanted to have this kind of conversation with my own daughter? Absolutely not! But here I am…in black and white trying to be as open as I can to help you."

"I'm sorry, daddy. It's just weird."

"Well, it ain't no walk in the park for me either suga, but nevertheless, it has to be talked about. Agreed?"

"Agreed."

"As long as I was thinking about creating images in my mind and desiring those women, I was never giving myself fully over to your mother. She no longer had my heart because delusions had it. Your mother told me to decide what I wanted because she couldn't compete any longer with those other women. Let me tell you how watching porn not only affects you but your spouse as well. It makes them feel inadequate, like they don't measure up, and they don't. You know why? Because they can never measure up to an illusion. It makes them question themselves, doubt themselves, which causes their confidence to falter. Trust me, if they don't feel confident with you, they will try to find someone else they feel comfortable with. There's nothing you can do or say about it because it was you that led them to it. When you try to hide it from them, you began lying to them, which breaks trust in the relationship. Do you have to clear out your phone and history so Grant doesn't see what you've been on?"

She put her head down in shame and said, "Yes."

"Have you lied to him about it?"

"Yes."

"Have you compared him to other men?"

"Yes."

"Is this the same reason why you won't go to church?"

Her eyes welled up, and she said, "God doesn't want me anymore. Look at what I've done. I wasn't raised this way, nor was it something I ever desired. I can't even explain the shame I feel."

"Shame comes with the territory. There's nothing about it that is good, and nothing good comes from it. The only thing that comes from porn is a "feel good" moment but a lifetime of shame, disappointment, sin, and condemnation. It can escalate more than what you've experienced already but don't allow it to keep you from getting the help you need."

"Where do I go to get help from this without feeling like a pervert?"

"Deliverance is never easy. It causes someone to take courageous steps to accept the wrong that was done and get help. The ones that stay behind closed doors and won't seek the help they know they need are cowards. It doesn't take strength to stay hidden. It takes strength to come out. I'm not going to tell you that you won't feel ashamed. I'm not going to tell you that you won't feel condemned. I won't tell you that you won't feel like you're the only one in the world with this problem. But what I can tell you is this; you can't go by your feelings. The enemy is going to play on them as much as you allow him. Your feelings will keep you bound up in chains and will never permit you to be free. I can't do it for you. Grant can't do it for you neither can your mother. If you really want to be free, it's something you are going to have to want and strive for yourself. So, I ask…are you ready to give it up?"

"Everything in me wants to give it up but for all the wrong reasons."

"And what reasons are those?"

"I only want to give it up because, for one, it's a sin against God. Two, it's tearing up my marriage, and three, it keeps me from church and loving God as I should. But there is still something in me that desires to keep watching it."

"I know how that feels. You want to stop, but something keeps pulling you to it, right?"

"Exactly. I mean, it doesn't even make me feel good anymore. I used to be excited about it, but now I just watch it because I can."

"Do you get the same feeling?"

"Every now and again, but it has to be a certain thing for me to get excited. Man, I can't believe I'm talking to you about this."

"I'm not all that comfortable either, but my desire to help you is stronger than the unsettling feeling I'm having, discussing this with you."

"I guess."

"Look, pumpkin, I know you think those are the wrong reasons to give it up, but those are the right reasons to give it up."

"Really, daddy? I mean…shouldn't my reasons be to give it up because I want to give it up and not because of anyone else? Shouldn't I be free because that's what I want for myself versus for everyone else?"

"Who cares what the reasons are just as long as you come out of it. You know it's not good for you. What more of a reason do you need?"

"I don't know. Maybe I'm overthinking it."

"We all do that sometimes. We give something more thought than we should and end up missing the purpose of the thing. Let your reasons be your own. Don't let anyone or what you think anyone should say your reasoning should be. It's all up to you, Steph."

"Daddy, that's what Grant calls me," Stephanie blushed.

"I know, sweetheart. Can I ask you a question?"

"I mean, yeah, good Lord, after this, I'm pretty sure you can ask me anything."

"Why did you go to these sites in the first place?"

"Now, daddy, that's where I draw the line. I cannot talk to you about….I'm just sayin'…that's a little too close for comfort."

"Well, can you talk about it with me?" Grant asked as he walked into the room with Mrs. Chase. Stephanie looked back to see Grant and also seeing the disappointment in her mother's eyes. She dropped her head, and Mrs. Chase walked over to her and held her in her arms. She said, "There's nothing to be ashamed about, my dear. We all have our hang-ups and sins to bear. I love you so much, and there's nothing you could ever do to make me stop loving you." Stephanie wept in her mother's arms. Her father wrapped his wife and his daughter in his arms. He motioned for Grant to come over and hold his wife. Once they all surrounded Stephanie, Mr. Chase began praying for her.

He prayed, "Father, we come to you now asking for Your help. Stephanie needs You right now. Please forgive us for all our sins knowingly and unknowingly in the name of Jesus. Father, help Stephanie to overcome the addiction to porn. Thank you for her husband, who called for assistance and back-up to save his wife from this iniquity. Thank you, Father, for saving me from it and my marriage, but now we call on You to save Grant and Stephanie's marriage in the name of Jesus. I command the spirit of lust and perversion to come out of my daughter. I command the spirit of inadequacy to come out of Stephanie. I command whatever is going on in their marriage before all this happened to be brought to the forefront in the name of Jesus. Get to the root of it, Jesus. I command my daughter to be totally and completely free from the spirit and addiction of porn, the immoral perversion of it, the sexual activity of it, and the lies, manipulation, and deceit of it. Father, please allow your peace to infiltrate her right now so she won't feel ashamed walking into Your church house in the name of Jesus. I command that she wins within her soul, in her marriage, and in her walk with You Jesus. Cause her to love you again and to desire you more than she desires porn. Let not her house be found empty when the spirits try to come back. Let them find her house to be full of Your love, Your joy, Your peace, Your strength, and most of all Your word in the name of Jesus we pray. Amen."

The family shared tears and clung to hope. They are in expectation that Stephanie is on the way to a courageous change. Throughout their visit, Stephanie was back in the kitchen with her mother like old times. She realized how much she missed home. She wasn't so sure about living in Jacksonville anymore. It brought nothing but pain. Nothing good came out of living there. She and Grant were always at odds with one another. Even her job at Le Floures was more stressful than she thought it would be, and it was taking its toll. She has many decisions she has to make, but this time with Grant by her side.

Chapter Twelve: The Road to Change

Mr. and Mrs. Chase left the hotel once they were finished talking and praying. Grant and Stephanie were left to discuss some of the issues they were having. Grant was fine with the prayer and all, but he was a tad bit disturbed that Stephanie could communicate more with her father than with him. She hadn't as so much divulged a reason why she was into porn. He wanted answers, and no one could give them to him but her.

They were quiet, but the tension had a voice. It was apparent to Grant that his wife had a better relationship or communication with her parents than with him. He could even talk to them better than he could with his own wife. He has the type of relationship with her parents that he strongly desired but lacked with his own. Mr. and Mrs. Chase had a way of making everyone around them feel comfortable. They carried and was the epitome of southern hospitality. He didn't know if he should fault his wife for that or not but wondered why some of that didn't rub off on her. She doesn't talk to him like she does with them. She doesn't communicate as openly with him as she does with them. He didn't know if he was jealous of that or what, but what he did know was he wanted that same type of relationship.

Stephanie decided to go and take a shower. While there, she thought about a lot of things. She wasn't even mad anymore. She made a choice to let go of everything and be who Grant married. She realized she had changed quite a bit since they said their vows. She didn't even know who she was anymore. She lost herself in everyone and everything else. In the shower, she took the time to pray…something she hadn't done in a long time. She prayed, "Lord, I'm so sorry for what I've done. I don't even know how I fell so far or why I left You the way I did, but I know I'm ready to come back home to You. I've been away far too long. I'm sorry for the sin I committed against you and against my body and against my marriage. I want to do better. I have to do better. Grant deserves better. I've been selfish, lustful, all about me, and disobedient to You. I don't know how You've allowed me to open my eyes day after day, but I thank you that You did, so I would have the chance to get right before You. I feel so bad for what I've done and how I treated you and my husband. You saved him, and I'm sure I've pushed him away in some form or fashion. I should have been the one to push him further to You, and I'm sorry. Please teach me to be a better wife. Please, I beg You to take away the manipulation and illusion that porn has seduced me with and no longer allow those images to be what turns me on but cause it to be Grant alone who turns me on. Show me. Lead me. Let Your word be a lamp unto my feet and light to my pathway. Show me how to be a better Christian and witness for You. I want to win souls for Your kingdom though I haven't been doing the best job. Let me make it up to You. I know I could never do enough, but I can try; in Jesus' name, I pray. Amen." Stephanie couldn't tell whether it was tears or steam from the shower that was running down her face, but it didn't matter. She wiped her face and got out of the shower. She felt the Lord tugging her heart to read Proverbs 31, which was the first thing she was going to do when she came out of the bathroom.

While Stephanie was in the shower, Grant decided to be the first one, as always, to break the ice. He wanted to know why Stephanie did what she did, why she doesn't communicate with him like she does with her parents, and why they are always at odds with one another.

There were two very different agendas going on here for when Stephanie would come out of the bathroom. She is ready for peace. He's prepared for war. She has her hand on the doorknob. He is sitting at the table adjacent to the bathroom tapping his fingernails on the table with an annoying rhythmic sound waiting for her to come out of the bathroom. She turned the knob. The time is approaching…the creaking of the knob turns…but then there was a knock at the door; Stephanie stayed in the bathroom while Grant answered the door. He looked through the peephole because he surely wasn't expecting anyone. It was one of the hotel's employees. Grant opened the door and said, "Yes, may I help you?" Stephanie couldn't hear the whole conversation, although she tried. All she knew is that she couldn't leave the bathroom while someone else walked into their room. She had no clue what this was about and was very curious. Who even knew they were there besides Arielya and her parents? After a few seconds, she heard the door close and asked Grant, "Is it okay to come out now?" He replied with a yes. She came out and looked at what had been done.

"What's all of this?" she asked.

"I didn't do any of this, but there's a note that came with it," said Grant.

"Well, what does it say?"

"It says, Grant and Stephanie, you all have been through some hard storms and will have more in the future, so now isn't the time to be against one another. It's time to be closer and strengthened by one another. Can you not see it? God is doing a new thing in you individually and as a married couple; now it shall spring forth; shall ye not know it? He will even make a way in the wilderness and rivers in the desert, according to Isa 43:19. Stephanie, Proverbs 31:11, the heart of her husband safely trust in her, so that he shall have no need of spoil and Grant, love your wife and be not bitter against her as it says in Colossians 3:19. I will end in Ephesians 5 to tell you two to submit yourselves one to another in the fear of God. Grant, you are to love Stephanie even as Christ loved the church and gave himself for it. As a man and husband, there will be times when you will have to give yourself for Stephanie. This is one of those times. It's time for both of you to let the word of Christ dwell in you richly in all wisdom; teaching and admonishing one another in psalms and hymns and spiritual songs, singing with grace in your hearts to the Lord just as Colossians 3:16 says. I know I usually joke around, but I didn't know how much I affected your marriage, which was never my intention. I really thought I was helping but didn't consider the harm it could cause. I'm sorry…so sorry. Love you guys – Arielya."

"Wow. All I can say is wow."

"I can't believe that is the same person. I would have never taken Arielya to be a person of the word at all. I mean, I know you'll grew up in church together, but I didn't know she was actually serious about it."

"There's a lot of things you don't know about Arielya. Yes, she jokes a lot, but she can be serious when she needs to be. It's the only way she copes with the heartache she went through in her childhood."

"Well, let's enjoy the chocolate covered strawberries and fruit she sent for us."

"I'm going to have to call her…"

"Uh, you ain't calling her till tomorrow."

"That's what I was going to say."

"Just making it plain."

"Speaking of Arielya, she said something today that kind of got under my skin."

"What was that?"

"She said it's a rumor that you cheated on me."

Grant was caught off guard, but his old instincts kicked in and how to deny and deflect this type of inquiry from any woman he dated without having to physically deny the allegations. Although he was shaken on the inside, he played it off. He said sarcastically, "And who is this person I supposedly slept with?"

"Ashley."

"The girl from the documentary?" he said as he laughed. Then he said, "You can't be serious. Where would people get that from?" He was stunned that it got out because he thought he was careful. She never stayed at his place, he never took her out anywhere, and he always went to her place at night.

"I just chalked it up to you guys working together on the documentary."

"Man, folk need to mind their own business, especially when they don't know what's going on. Folk always running off at the mouth. You don't believe that, do you?"

"No, but I wouldn't be me if I didn't ask," she said as she had this look on her face trying to fill him out and meaning business.

"I'm glad you know me, though."

"But let me clear, it would not be a good thing for you if you eva in your life decide to cheat on me."

"For real? It's like that?"

"Facts! Straight 100."

"You crazy."

"You don't want to know that side of me. You've been very fortunate, and I'd advise you keep it that way."

"You don't have to worry but let me address what got under my skin."

"Yeah, and what's that?"

"Arielya did say something that stuck out."

"What?"

"She said it's her fault. What's her fault?"

"I talked to her about what I had been doing and told her that if it wasn't for her "advice," I never would have started watching porn in the first place."

"What was her advice? What did y'all talk about?"

"After our honeymoon, I told her that I was feeling inadequate about having sex with you."

"Why?"

"Because I was a virgin, and you had been with plenty of women. I couldn't measure up to that, and apparently, I didn't bring much to the table?"

"You didn't have to bring anything except the love you have for me. That's all I wanted, Steph."

"Yeah, you say that, but do you know how many marriages fail because of the lack of being satisfied? I didn't want that to happen to us, so I did what I felt like I had to keep you happy and us together."

"No, what you lacked was knowledge about the whole sex thing. It sounds like you listened to a bunch of cackling hens who knows nothing about it. The marriages don't fall apart because of the lack of being satisfied. It falls apart because the two involved in the marriage lacked the meaning of what sex really is."

"And what's that? Please tell me."

"Don't be sarcastic. I'm telling you what I know. Sex isn't about just the bedroom. It's so much more to it than that. I learned that from you. I didn't fall in love with you because sex was involved; I fell in love because there was more to you than just that. I had my fill of lifeless and loveless sex. It's not fulfilling and leaves you lonely, believe me, I know. But you, Steph, you are my total package. Sex is the ice cream on the cake. Making love starts before the bedroom comes into play. Anybody can have sex. That has been proven, but it doesn't keep a relationship going. If anyone measures their marriage on sex only, then they've already lost, and it's doomed from the beginning."

"But you can't lie about it. Sex is a huge part of marriage."

"Yes, it's a part of marriage, but let me ask you something. What happens if something happens and a husband or wife becomes paralyzed? What do spouses and their soldiers do during a fifteen-month deployment? What happens if that husband can't perform due to stress? What if a woman can't commit to sex because of surgery? What then?"

"I…I don't know."

"So, you mean to tell me it is okay for a marriage to fail because one of them has lost the ability to perform?"

"No, I'm not saying it's right, but what I am saying is that has to be a struggle. We all have needs."

"You didn't have that need nor focused on that need before we were married."

"Yes, because waiting for marriage was important to me."

"So, how is it any different from those other situations?"

"Once you have sex, you have urges."

"Didn't you have some of those very same urges when you were a virgin?"

"Yes. Urges don't stop just because you are a virgin."

"Exactly. Again, what's the difference?"

"You are backing me into a corner."

"No, I'm not. I'm asking you legitimate questions and proving a point."

"And what point is that?"

"Was our relationship important to you before marriage?"

"You know it was."

"Was physical intimacy involved?"

"No."

"But you and I were both willing to do what we had to do to make it work, right?"

"Yes."

"And we both decided to wait right…even though it was a struggle for me."

"I know it was hard for you, which is exactly my point. You struggled with it, and it was because you were having sex with other women before me."

"Meaningless sex. Nothing worth having. I dealt with materialistic females. I thought that was what I liked and wanted and what I needed, but you proved me wrong, Steph. That husband or wife I mentioned earlier needs the support of their spouse. They need to feel loved. They need to feel secure. I'm sure they already feel some type of way about not being able to be intimate with their spouse, but the pressure from the other to perform isn't fair either. This is why sex can't be a basis for marriage. Sometimes you will be satisfied, and sometimes you won't be. No one is satisfied every time they lie down and have sex. Does that mean the marriage is over? I hope not because if so, the marriage wasn't based on anything concrete or foundational anyway."

"Seems like I have a lot to learn then cause that doesn't make sense to me."

"If you feel like sex is the only thing that is going to hold us together, then we won't make it, Steph. We will end up right back here in this place again." Grant was exasperated and said, "I'm going to bed."

"Baby, I'm sorry. I don't mean it like that."

"Steph, our communication should not be based on sex. It should be based on Christ, respect, honor, verbal communication, and love for one another. You have totally missed the whole point of this conversation. We'll talk in the morning, but for now, I'm going to bed. Goodnight."

"Come on, Grant. Don't be like that. Make me understand. Help me."

"Get in the bed, and we'll talk in the morning. I love you. Goodnight," Grant said as he kissed her on the forehead.

Stephanie was puzzled. She felt even worse. She climbed in the bed as Grant requested. She thought maybe she could change his mood by her coming on to him. She tried to arouse him, but he was not turned on at all. He responded to her advances by saying, "See, this is what I'm talking about. You can't fix this with sex. Your love communication has changed severely. I love you, Stephanie, but go to sleep." She rolled over, not saying a word. He wrapped his body about hers to cuddle to make her feel secure in his love for her. She wept quietly. She didn't want him to know she was crying. He hated to see her cry. She kept sniffing, which let him know she was crying. He asked her, "Are you crying?" She answered, "No." He slowly reached for her face to wipe her tears. Then he said, "Come here, my sexy lady." She rolled over towards him, and he held onto her. "I'm not mad at you, Steph. I just want more for us, that's all." She nodded her head and cried herself to sleep, realizing she didn't know much about marriage at all. She focused so much on keeping her virginity and saving herself for marriage that she forgot to prepare it.

Chapter Thirteen: G.O.A.L. Gem of a Lady

The next morning, Stephanie woke up alone. She looked around for Grant but couldn't find him. He left his phone, so she knew he couldn't be far. It gave her the time she needed to reread Arielya's note and read Proverbs 31.

Once she read Proverbs 31, she didn't fully understand what it meant, so she began studying the verses one by one. She knew this was going to be a process and that it wasn't going to happen overnight, so she carefully dissected the question in verse ten," Who can find a virtuous woman?" Stephanie heard this scripture time and time again during the women conferences and at Women's Day at church. However, she figured there had to be more to it than what was taught since she still had no clue what a virtuous woman is and sinking in her own marriage. She asked God, "What does it mean, Lord? When I look at the definition of virtuous, which means righteous, good, pure, angelic, ethical, upright, and exemplary, I've failed in every area. How can I live up to that? Once again, I'm found inadequate. I'm going to fail at this every time." She felt God impress upon her heart, saying, "The world put those expectations on you, not Me. If you look up My definition of virtuous, you'll find that it describes something totally different. I define virtuous as strength, wealthy, powerful, and efficient. That is how I made women. It doesn't mean to be domineering. It means that she's wealthy in strength and powerful and efficient in Spirit. Being strong doesn't necessarily mean leading; it could also mean being strong enough to follow when she needs to. She's wealthy as in possessing the fruit of the spirit. It doesn't mean she can't be wealthy monetarily, but those kinds of riches wither away. The wealth that the Proverbs 31 woman possess continues to eternity. It can't be bought, and this is why she is worth far more than rubies. She is powerful in the Spirit because prayer is her weapon. She's undefeated because I'm her source. It may seem like she loses some battles, but that's not the case. It's just not going the way one would want, but the war is won. She is efficient because her faith keeps her going. She knows who I AM, who she belongs to, and what I'm capable of and more than able to do."

After she wrote down all that the Lord was speaking, she was full as if she had a breakfast platter. She prayed after ending her study and got herself ready for the day. Grant walked through the door as she put on her last bit of clothing.

"Where have you been?" Stephanie asked.

"Good morning to you," Grant said.

"Yeah, yeah, good morning. Where have you been?"

"Can I at least get a good morning kiss first?"

"I didn't get mine before you left."

"Yes, you did. I gave you a kiss on the forehead before I left."

"Oh."

"Yeah, that's right! Now beg my forgiveness."

"What! Boy, you must be crazy."

"I am King!"

"Please…stick your bird chest back in."

"Oh, you weren't saying that when you were drooling the first time you saw my chest."

"Whatever."

"Oh, so you sayin' if I take off my shirt right now, you won't stare?"

"Why you gotta be acting like that?"

"I'm just sayin'."

"See, I got a fresh word from heaven, then you come up in here picking with me."

"Awh, look at my baby, learning her Bible. You deserve a kiss."

"Deserve? You didn't know you are not your own but been bought with a price. I can take what I want."

"I like the sound of that."

"Yeah, I'm sure you do."

"Keep speaking the word to me, baby."

"You are crazy. Are you going to tell me where you've been or what?"

"Or what?"

"I see you woke up clowning today. Just a hee hee, haw haw funny."

"Naw, I'm playing. I went to go talk to my spiritual father."

"How is Pastor Garnett doing?"

"He's good. He was glad to see me."

"I'm sure."

"We were talking about stuff, man to man."

"That's cool. I'm glad you have someone you can talk to like that."

"I wish it could be my father who I could talk to, but you know how that goes."

"Yeah. I know. When was the last time you talked to him?"

"Our wedding. I'm surprised he showed."

"What happened between you two? You don't talk about it much."

"If I knew, I could tell it to you, but I don't. All I know is we were close, then once he and my mom split so did he. I guess since we were grown, he didn't feel like he needed to continue to be a father. I don't know, Steph. Onto better things…get ready, so we can go grab something to eat."

They headed out for the day and hung out with her parents. Grant decided to stop by his mother's house and even his father's. He has wanted to speak with him for a long time to figure out the problem and why he doesn't stay in contact with him. His visit to his mother's house was pleasant. She reaches out to Grant regularly. She loves her daughter-in-law but doesn't know what they are going through because Grant has not disclosed that to her and decided not to. She started dating again, and Grant got to meet the new man in her life. He was sort of a brat about it. He didn't like seeing his mother with another man. He didn't want her with his dad either, especially after what he put her through. Stephanie was embarrassed by the way he was acting. She kicked his leg, pinched his arm, and stepped on his foot to get him to behave himself. Grant paid it no mind. He wasn't digging his mother being with someone else. It just didn't feel right. His mother wasn't pleased about it either. She pulled him into the kitchen and gave him a piece of her mind. She's nowhere near saved, so her conversation with him was brash, to say the least. She explained to him that she deserves to move on and be happy again. She doesn't plan on walking down the aisle any time soon, but she has every right to get back out there. She told him that she lived her life for them and her ex-husband,

and everyone has moved on except her, and that wasn't fair. When she spoke this to Grant, he understood, didn't like it but understood. He apologized to the gentlemen and continued the visit with his mother.

The next morning Stephanie woke up early and studied a few more scriptures from Proverbs 31. She entitled it "The Heart of Her Husband." The Lord spoke to her heart, teaching her, "There is nothing worse than broken trust, especially when it comes to a man. He likes to feel secure, just like a woman. He wants to know the woman he chose to marry can be trusted, and when he finds her lacking in that area, he classifies her as "everyone else." It's just as hard to win back his trust as it is for a woman. It's already hard for a man to trust, and when it is broken, he feels like he has to take on things himself. When the scripture says that he shall have no need of spoil, it means he will not have any reason to doubt you and have suspensions about you because he fully trusts you. Don't create a doubt nor become suspicions. You create an unsettling atmosphere in your marriage when you do that. Your husband should be able to confidently say, "I know my wife," when someone tries to say something different about her. This is created by keeping nothing hidden. Share your heart. Honor his thoughts. Be truthful. Be honest. Respect your marriage and cut off all ties that will cause him to question your character and integrity. If he raises an eyebrow, it is a caution or warning sign doubt is creeping in, and that is not what you want. Make sure your marriage bond is neatly tied with strength, honor, and reverence…that 3-strong cord that's not easily broken."

Each day, God taught Stephanie another lesson from the Proverbs 31 chapter. She titled this lesson. Day three, God taught her about "No Need," Prov 31:12 *She will do him good and not evil all the days of her life.* God said, "We know what good is but what is considered evil? It's not just the big stuff like cheating and lying. It's hiding things from him, trying to control him, demeaning him, talking down to him or at him, dishonor, disrespect, keeping the "goodies" away from him because you're mad at him, teaching the children to disrespect him (whether verbally or by watching), taking advantage of the finances; evil is anything that will cause him to look at you in a different light by something you said or did. A wife adds to her husband's life, just like he is supposed to add to hers. There shouldn't be any subtraction or division in a marriage, only adding and multiplying. Her being good to him doesn't end at his life; it ends at hers. Speak well of your husband. Treat him good, and nothing will be withheld from you."

Day four, God gave her the title, "This Woman Works" from verses 13-19 *"She seeketh wool, and flax, and worketh willingly with her hands. 14 She is like the merchant's ships; she bringeth her food from afar. 15 She riseth also while it is yet night, and giveth meat to her household, and a portion to her maidens. 16 She considereth a field, and buyeth it: with the fruit of her hands, she planteth a vineyard. 17 She girdeth her loins with strength, and strengtheneth her arms. 18 She perceiveth that her merchandise is good: her candle goeth not out by night. 19 She layeth her hands to the spindle, and her hands hold the distaff."* He said, "She speaks without speaking. She's not using her mouth to keep her busy, but she's using her hands. She's not seeking out other people's business; instead, she's seeking those things that will help her build her household. As a wife, Stephanie, you have to use your hands…willingly…to build up your house. Make sure your family is properly clothed and healthy. Use those things (with your hands) to work diligently in turning items I've given you to create great things for your household. If you don't know how then learn. There are plenty of classes and videos you can watch which will teach you how to do it. You may not know how to do all things, but you can learn some things to help hold your home together. You have the chef cooking down pat, but you could really be strengthened in other areas. Don't be intimidated by what you do not know. Get motivated to learn how so you will be able to do more. It takes a coward to only focus on his or her strength, but it takes a courageous person to admit they do not know and learn so they can be strengthened in their weaknesses. This woman that works is wise when it comes to the field she wants to work in, and she buys into it. She sows into it or invests. Then she takes what she invested in and uses it to plant a vineyard or in a place within her own land, so it can grow and give her and her family what they need. She doesn't allow it to become dormant. There will be rough days, but it's in those rough days her arms will be strengthened. The Proverbs 31 woman is not just a mystical character in some random book. She's an example of how I designed you to be. I'm not asking you to be perfect, but I do expect you to perfect My plan for your life. Sometimes, women do not know their own strength. Stephanie, you are a strong woman. I designed you that way. In no way are you weak and feeble. I have strengthened your arms, and you can do battle. It says she perceives her merchandise is good. That just means she's confident. She doesn't need reassurance about her gift and what I have given her to do. She's confident in Me and how I provide for her. She knows what I have placed in her lap, and no one can tell her different. I'm not saying she's cocky, but I am saying she's confident, a humble and strong woman on all fronts. She can multi-task and does what is necessary to get the job done. Don't always wait on Me to give you the go-ahead. Consider what is before you on all accounts, then make a decision. You have to know that I am with you wherever you go. I'm not going to lead you wrong. If I see you headed in a direction that is not from Me, then I will intervene, but Stephanie, you have to make a move. Don't wait around any longer. Consider the field and plant your vineyard."

Day five, Stephanie learned, "She's Compassionate" from verse twenty, *"She stretcheth out her hand to the poor; yea, she reacheth forth her hands to the needy."* Stephanie prayed, "Father, I do this already. I am compassionate." God said to her, "I know you are because that is how I created you. How do you spell compassionate? W-O-M-A-N. You are a woman of compassion and love. Do not let anyone tell you that you're an angry or bitter woman who doesn't know how to treat a man, nor that you do not need one because I created you to be a nurturing being. Everything about you screams nurturer and love. I built you to learn to help those that are in need. It pulls on the very nature of you. Have you noticed how you nurture anyone, and they don't have to be close to you or even know you? It's because it's who you are. The world wants you to stop caring and nurturing. They are trying to redefine the role of the woman. Do know this; they can't because who you really are will spill out of you. You are a helper, and you help those in need. This is who you are; embrace it. It doesn't mean to let people run all over you; on the contrary, be wise in helping and who you help and if it's the right time. Sometimes I will give it to you not to help someone because I know more about their situation than what they are telling you. Trust how I lead you. Guard your heart by placing Me as the guard versus a wall. Being a compassionate nurturer is far from selfish. It is an extension beyond yourself. Remember who you are, and you will go further than you ever thought you'd go."

Stephanie was enjoying the time she was spending with the Lord. She felt herself getting back to "normal." Grant watched his wife learn more about who she really is day by day. He wouldn't bother her at all. He allowed God to teach her without his input. Grant understood this was crucial to their marriage.

On day six, she continued to learn more. This day the Lord talked to her about "Winter Coverage" from verses 21-22 *"She is not afraid of the snow for her household: for all her household are clothed with scarlet. 22 She maketh herself coverings of tapestry; her clothing is silk and purple."* God said, "When a woman has her household together, she doesn't worry about the "winter" time. The winter time also means hard times. You can't look at this only in the natural Stephanie. You have to see with your spiritual eyes as well. She doesn't just have her natural home taken care of, but she also has her spirit in check too. She knows how to clothe her family. She is like the ant who prepares for the winter months. The seasons never change. There will always be a fall, winter, spring, and summer, so it is easy to prepare for that season. She makes sure the pantry and fridge are stocked. She shops smart, getting more bang for her buck. When winter strikes, she doesn't have to worry. She can be confident in how she previously prepared for it. Stephanie, the Proverbs 31 woman takes her spirituality with just as much tenacity as she does for her household. She not only needs to know how to handle her home naturally, but she also needs to prepare herself for any spiritual "winters" that come. She has to be spiritually minded to manage her husband's trials and how it affects the family. She has to deal with her children's immaturity and the things they get themselves into, financial woes, and even the things she goes through herself without losing who she is, a woman of God. How is this done? She seeks me early in the morning. She listens and obeys My every instruction. She studies My word and allows the Holy Spirit to lead her into revelation. She makes sure she fasts when instructed by Me. She does the things needed to get close to Me. She is more concerned about having a relationship with Me than building other relationships that are not guaranteed to last. This is not to say that she doesn't mess up from time to time, but when she does, she knows how to get it right with Me…and that's what's important! Stephanie, learn from her. Take what you can from her and build it to where it works for you. I'm not asking you to be perfect; I'm asking you for a relationship with Me."

Day number seven totally blew her mind. Stephanie was in awe of what she learned. It gave her life. Her eyes were opened, and something in her heart clicked. She realized the significance of "Representation" from Proverbs 31:23, *"Her husband is known in the gates, when he sitteth among the elders of the land."* God said, "I know this doesn't seem like it should be here, but it's actually essential. **YOU REPRESENT YOUR HUSBAND!** Upholding your husband is more than "speaking life" to him; it's showing others he's taking care of the home. People watch how a husband takes care of his wife by what she does and how she carries herself. This is the reason other women go after another woman's husband because they want what you've been graced and blessed to have. Ask yourself, Stephanie, how have you been representing your husband? He's known in the gates and sits among the elders, but what is the perception because of you? You leave him to go to church by himself. The pastor wants to elevate him but can't because you refuse to get in place. You lie to him about the sin you know you commit. He hasn't been happy for some time now, and other women can smell it. I don't say this to invoke fear. I say it to make you step up your game and become who I created you to be for him. **I MADE YOU FOR HIM!** You are his rib, but right now, he's in pain because his "rib" is broken. It's time for you to get back on your horse and represent yourself as a virtuous woman. You can't continue to walk around broken and continuously think he's going to mend your wounds. If he does, he will become a broken man, and someone who is broken gets tired of fixing the next person. When he looks at you, what does he see? If he always sees a problem, he will always see pain, someone he has to fix. You continue to approach him about an issue, and he tries to fix it, but **YOU WON'T LET HIM.** How then is he supposed to feel? If you are always helping someone and they continuously reject you or the advice you are giving, what do you do? Then why would you expect him to do anything less? Covenant or not, people get tired of always having to fix other people.

Therefore, what you do now is going to be left up to you. Will you continue to wallow in your sin or hold onto hurt you said you let go of, or will you come to Me and allow for Me to heal you so you, in turn, can heal your marriage? He is known in the gates…but how is he known through you?

Not only do you represent him, but you also represent Me. I am your Father. I am the one who presented you to Grant. When you are not representing him, how do you think that makes Me look? I take care of my own, and I need you to take care of what I have blessed you with and honor that covenant. You cannot walk around shying away from Me or the ministry I have called you and Grant to. It's time to get yourself together. No more excuses. No more stalling. No more pity parties. Make it happen as I always make everything happen for you."

After this devotion, Stephanie thought about her wardrobe, her hair, her attitude, lies, failures, sins, and her marriage. She could either wallow in it or change it as the Father has said. What was she going to do? How was she going to do this because it's hard to get up from a fall? Regardless, she knew she had to make a change. It is already in motion. Now she has to put actions with her prayers. However, to make this drastic change, she had to finish up the chapter.

The next day, she learned "Woman of Business" from verse twenty-four, *"She maketh fine linen, and selleth it; and delivereth girdles unto the merchant."* God said, "Being a virtuous woman is not just about being a wife, a mother, and taking care of her home. It's also making sure she utilizes the gift(s) I have given her. She doesn't bury her talents. She causes it to increase. She's a businesswoman. She makes money for herself. Her joy is in the things she's able to do for herself. It ultimately benefits her household, but her life isn't only geared towards only doing for her home.

This is something that can never be taken away from her. It's like cooking for you. You will soon open your own restaurant, but as of now, you're making it work for you. Cooking is your gift, your talent, and you're not burying it. You're constantly using it and blessing others with the food you cook. You can even sell dinner plates or host a small catering company until you open your own restaurant."

"But Lord, I've never thought about that," Stephanie said.

"I know, which is why I'm revealing it to you now. It will be a ways away, but you can prepare for it. Cooking brings you joy, does it not?"

"Yes, it does," Stephanie replied.

"Why does it bring you joy?"

"Because it reminds me of home and cooking with my mom. I love cooking and creating new dishes then watching the reactions of those tasting my food."

"Never let your gift go to waste. It's what I've given you, and no one can take that away from you. To continue working your talent, keep yourself in shape. Exercise. Eat right because it takes a lot to do what you do. Do not allow your passion to diminish due to others and mostly to sin. Keep the creativity of your talent flowing by increasing your relationship with Me. Everything always flows back to Me. It's the way you operate. It's the way you move. It's your way of life."

Day ten was about "Strength and Honor" from verses 25-28, *"Strength and honour are her clothing and she shall rejoice in time to come. She openeth her mouth with wisdom; and in her tongue is the law of kindness. She looketh well to the ways of her household, and eateth not the bread of idleness. Her children arise up, and call her blessed; her husband also, and he praiseth her.”* God said, “I really want to get into this one, Stephanie. It’s going to be life to you. Strength and honor are her clothing. This speaks volumes. It shows that not everything goes “right” for her. She’s not perfect. Her life is not perfect, but she carries it all with strength and with honor. She doesn’t fold. She’s human and makes mistakes. She knows her time will come to rejoice. She is secure in knowing she wins and has the victory. When you can come from that standpoint, you won’t be shaken. It’s about being confident in My word and in My promises. She could cuss people out. She could give people a piece of her mind. She could be vengeful. She could repay evil for evil. She could backstab someone. She could do all of that, but what would it accomplish? Instead, she chooses to speak with wisdom and kindness.

It’s not something she has to do, but it’s something she chooses to do, and that’s the difference. Throughout her life, she could be mad at plenty of things and have every right to act out, but she is confident in Me. She trusts Me. She looks to bless her home, not tear it down. This woman is not going to put her household through turmoil. She makes sure the atmosphere is set and is conducive to living life fulfilled. This is **HUGE....SHE...IS...NOT...IDLE**! She’s not sitting around eating bonbons and lying around on the couch. She’s not leaving her house a mess. She is always doing something productive. Being idle brings nothing but trouble and invites the devil to come lurking. That’s all he enjoys seeing. It’s all he needs to start some mess. You can’t give him a foothold. Remember, he comes to steal, kill, and destroy but also remember I came that you may have life and have it more abundantly. Idling is what caused you to enter into the sin of pornography. Idling gives your mind time to create situations that are not there; though it may have some merit, you can't give into it. Talk about it with your husband. You don't think the virtuous woman had struggles? Well, she did! It's how she overcomes them that makes her virtuous. She is not above anyone. Her family praises her and calls her blessed. Why? Not because she's perfect but because she's balanced, honorable, strong, and wise and is led by her Spirit instead of her flesh."

Day eleven was the last day, and she was ready to put things into practice. The last day summed up was about "Excelling" from verses 29-31, *"Many daughters have done virtuously, but thou excellest them all. Favour is deceitful, and beauty is vain: but a woman that feareth the LORD, she shall be praised. Give her of the fruit of her hands; and let her own works praise her in the gates."* The Father said, "The fear of the Lord is the beginning of knowledge, and it's the purest form of reverence. One thing a virtuous woman doesn't have to do, and that is to boast about who she is, what I'm doing in her life, bragging about all her blessings to throw in another woman's face and walk in pride. No, I'm all she needs. She allows Me to bring the noise. She allows her works to praise her. Beauty is fleeting, and it doesn't stay for long; it's temporary. She doesn't put stock in her beauty (even though she takes excellent care of herself). She puts her stock and herself all into Me. Through all this, Stephanie, I want you to see the relationship you so desperately need with Me. You are more than welcome to do it all without Me because I'm not going to force you but tell Me, how has it worked for you so far? What kind of bind are you in? Are you really where you want to be? These are things you have to ask yourself. Remember, being virtuous isn't about being perfect. It's knowing that you aren't but striving to be. I hope our studies have helped you and that you make a choice to renew our relationship. You will have to make a choice, and I just hope that choice is Me. I love you, daughter."

Stephanie thought long and hard over everything the Lord had shown her. She knew this wasn't going to be easy, and it would require a lot of work. It seemed to be more work than she's capable of, but none-the-less she decided to choose the Lord and change the atmosphere of her home.

Chapter Fourteen: Let Virtuosity Begin

It's their last day in Savannah, and Grant wants to visit his father before they leave in hopes of changing their relationship for the better. Plus, he had questions about his unknown siblings. They left to go to his father's house. It wasn't a nice visit. For one, it took Mr. Bennet five knocks and constant doorbell ringing for him to come to the door. They knew he was home because they saw his car in the driveway. They were kind of shocked at the upkeep of his house. He didn't seem to care for his lawn or curb appeal at all. This is not at all like his father. He remembers his dad as clean-cut…everything clean and in its place.

Mr. Bennet finally answered the door and said, "Who is it ringing my doorbell like that!"

"It's me pops, Grant," he said.

Mr. Bennet unlocked the door and said, "It's good to see you, son, but you know I don't like to be bothered on my day off."

"I didn't know it was your day off," Grant said.

"Well, now, you know. Have a seat. You and…what's your name again, dear?" Mr. Bennet asked.

"Stephanie, sir," she said, feeling insulted.

"I'm sorry, baby, but I'm not good with names," Mr. Bennet said, but Stephanie didn't even dignify it with a response.

"What have you been up to, pops?" Grant asked.

"Working and coming home. I ain't got time for nothing else. I gotta keep up with these alimony payments. You think child support is bad…it ain't got nothing on alimony payments. Your momma needs to get remarried quick, fast, and in a hurry," Mr. Bennet said.

Grant wanted to reply with harsh words but decided to keep his mouth shut. They weren't there long and already wanted to leave. Mr. Bennet didn't make them feel welcomed and wanted them to go just as bad as they did. The more they conversed, the more Grant became unglued. He said, "You know, Pops, I came over here thinking…"

"Well, that's the first thing you did wrong…think," Mr. Bennet said, cutting Grant off.

"You know what forget it. I guess we will never have the relationship we once had, and I'm just about over it."

"I don't know what to tell you, son."

"Bye, Pops," Grant said as he left his father's house. Mr. Bennet didn't even budge. He closed the door and headed back to watching television in his room, lying on his bed. Grant didn't even get a chance to ask about his other family; he didn't care at this point. He doesn't know them, so he can keep going with his life without knowing them.

Stephanie wanted to console Grant, but she knew when it came to his father, there wasn't much she could do or that he would allow her to do. That was just a hole she didn't want to go down. As they drove away, Grant's face was still, no emotion. Then he said, "I don't know what happened. I have no clue why he's turned so cold."

"Have you ever asked him?" Stephanie asked.

"I didn't think I had to. He is old enough to act like an adult and actually be a parent. He's the one who stepped out. It should be my mother who is bitter, but she is living life."

"Is he still with the woman he left your mom for?"

"I don't know, but I guess not cause it doesn't look like he has much of a life."

"Maybe he's living in regret. Did you ever think about that?"

"If that's the case, then wouldn't he try to mend the relationship instead of destroying it more?"

"I don't know. Emotions affect people in different ways."

"Don't care and don't want to talk about it anymore."

"Okay," Stephanie said.

It was time for Grant and Stephanie to head back home. They said their good-byes and headed towards home. Stephanie left Savannah with her spirits lifted, her man on her arm, and her soul intact. There was something different this time about her leaving porn alone altogether. She knew it wasn't going to be easy, but she knew she could handle it for some reason.

Grant was somewhat different, though. He took his father's visit hard. Stephanie could tell he was still bothered about what happened. The ride home was quiet between the two, and Stephanie felt one of the lessons she learned coming into play. She prayed inwardly, "Father, I don't know what to do about Grant. His father really hurt him. The last time he did that, Grant did things that weren't good. Father, what can I do to alleviate the pain? Show me how to minister to him right now that will change his mood and uplift his spirit?" God lead her to play his favorite movie on her tablet. She went to one of his favorite parts, made sure the volume was up and played the movie. She pressed play, and when the scene was done, Grant busted out with a loud laugh. Stephanie just watched him laugh for a few seconds because it was what he needed. Then they looked at each other and started laughing. He told her to rewind it and play it again three times. The Lord spoke to her heart, "Laughter frees the soul." She replied with a thank you Lord.

They arrived home. Once they unpacked, Stephanie asked Grant to sit down with her to discuss some changes she's making. He agreed to sit with her. She said, "I'm going to need your help. It's going to be hard, which is why I am going to need you. I can't do this on my own. First of all, I want to ask your forgiveness for misrepresenting you and lying to you. I'm sorry. Please forgive me."

"Already have. What do you need me to do?"

"For one, I found this website and app that will watch over me while I'm on my phone and laptop. I need you to upload it and put in a password and do not give it to me. It will alert you if I try to go to a porn site."

"Okay. That's no problem."

"I want us to pray about a few things."

"And what's that?"

"One is moving back home, and the other is me quitting my job for right now. I just feel like I need to be home and working on our marriage and putting home first, but I also want to start working on opening my own restaurant."

"Moving back to Savannah? Yeah, we will have to pray about that. I'm making traction at the lab, and I don't want to mess that up. Then quitting your job? I understand what you're saying but finding a less demanding job is better because we need the money right now. We can't afford for neither one of us to stop working or you opening your own restaurant. I want to help you own your own business. Let's look into the cost, requirements, take business classes, and gain all the information first. Then we can then proceed with opening your restaurant. Plus, we don't know if we're going to move or not, and I think that is going to be key in opening your business."

"I guess you're right. I just know my job will continue to keep me out of church, and I don't want that. I want to be with you."

"I get that, and I want that too, but financially, we can't swing that right now. How about this, we will pray about it as you suggested and let God reveal to us what we need to do, but until then, we keep doing what we have been doing until He releases us or tells us something different. While we are waiting, we can put money aside, so when God says go, we can without it killing us financially."

"Okay. That's fair."

"I'm proud of you."

"Awh, thanks, bae."

Stephanie returned to work, and Grant returned to his job. When she got back, her supervisor sat down to have a talk with her. He said, "Stephanie, you don't know how close you came to losing your job. I understand you had a family emergency, but you were gone for almost two weeks, and you just can't be out of place for that long. I didn't want to do this, but I need you to sign this infraction report. You can read it over and sign it or not, but if you don't, you won't have a job." Stephanie was shocked. She'd never had a bad report written up on her…ever. She knew this was a consequence of her sin, so she laid her pride to the side, signed the report, and apologized to her supervisor. Stephanie went back to work doing what she loved. God revealed to her, a virtuous woman admits her mistakes and change, and she doesn't get upset about the consequences she created. She deals with it because she knows God's grace is sufficient. It didn't feel good, but Stephanie knew there wasn't anything she could do about it.

After being back at work for a few months, she noticed she began to fall back into the same things before her revelatory revelations. She couldn't get to church because of her hectic schedule. She was barely at home and could hardly call her husband. She couldn't do it anymore. She refused to go back. She sat down with her supervisor and asked if she could have Sundays off. She was working way too much. The turnover rate was frequent, which made her job more challenging. She was working double shifts at least three times every week. He agreed to give her every other Sunday off, but there wasn't any money in the budget to hire nor promote someone else. Stephanie didn't like it, but she took whatever leverage she could.

Grant was excited to have his wife to go to church with him every other Sunday versus not at all. It was still a strain on their marriage. They hardly saw each other. Whenever Stephanie would get home from work, she was exhausted and would fall out on the bed. They were barely having relations; conversation was minimum, and stress was at an all-time high.

One day, Grant was at work, and someone came through the door he least expected. She said, "Hi, Grant." He looked at her and looked around and said, "What are you doing here?" She said, "Is that what you say to your wife?"

"I'm sorry. I just didn't expect to see you here, especially when I know you're supposed to be at work."

"I wanted to surprise you. I'm off today, sooo…"

"For real?"

"Yes. Can you break away for a little bit?"

Grant smiled and said, "For you, I would like to take off the rest of the day, but I can step away for a little bit."

Stephanie grinned and said, "Let's go."

They went out on a picnic. She laid out a blanket under a huge tree near a lake at the park that was minutes away from where he worked. She played some R&B music softly from her phone, then arranged the food she set out. They talked and laughed, and it was good. She laid between his legs and smiled, but it was time for Grant to return to work. Before getting out of the car, Stephanie said, "I wish we could go to a bed and breakfast."

"Why can't we?"

"You have to go back to work."

"We always have this weekend."

"Cool, let's go."

The weekend came quickly, and they were ready to spend the weekend together. Stephanie drove to the bed and breakfast resort. Grant was finally enjoying his wife as he envisioned. It had been a hard road. He wanted to get her to exercise, take better care of herself, and give her a different outlook to where she's not focused on getting over her sin and its struggle. When they pulled up in front of the bed and breakfast, Grant asked her, "Is this where we're staying the night?"

"Yes, is that going to be a problem?"

"No, but how much did this cost?"

"Don't worry about it. I got us covered," she said while they walked in, checked in, and got settled.

"How long have you been planning this?"

"Since Wednesday. I talked with my supervisor and told him that I needed some time off. I'd been working every single day for months, and it just can't be that way. He knew he was wrong for that. He agreed to let me have a couple of days off. I'm glad I at least got a consistent day off on Sundays cause other than that, I'm drained. It's just too much."

"I'll admit it is a bit much. I don't know how they expect anybody to work like that."

"That's this business. They don't pay enough for that, but at least with the extra hours, we have been able to put away a few thousand dollars so far."

"Yeah, that has been the plus side to it all."

"Has God said anything to you about us moving back to Savannah or me quitting?"

"No, it's been quiet. I've been asking."

"Me too but nothing."

"Well, as long as He isn't saying anything, then we keep doing what we're doing."

"But is that God? We haven't been able to spend any time together, and the stress has been…man…do I even need to say?"

"You're right, but I don't think it's His will for us to stop moving while we're waiting on an answer. I believe this is a faith thing. Faith is trusting He is hearing our prayers, and He's working on our behalf even though we don't see it or feel it. I know you're tired, babe, so am I, but we have to keep going until something changes or when that answer comes."

"I guess so."

"We're not here in this beautiful room to talk about that but to enjoy each other, right?"

"You're right. I'm sorry.

"You good, babe. But I tell you what I want to do right now."

"And what's that?"

He walked up on her, picked her up, she wrapped her legs around him, and he kissed her. She said, "Oh, so you want to get right to it, huh?" He said, "You got a problem with that?" She answered, "What do you think?"

Once they finished making love, they laid in bed under the covers and talked. Stephanie said, "I don't know if this is the right time to talk about this, but I want to tell you something I'd been struggling with since making changes in my life and the testimony of right now."

Grant said, "Ooookay…"

"I don't know if you're going to look at me differently, though."

"Just say it. You have to be able to talk to me. If you can't talk to me, who can you talk to?"

"I know, but it's kind of embarrassing, and I'm kinda ashamed."

"Babe, if it is something that's on your heart, then you have to trust that God gave it to you at this moment."

"Okay…well…here it goes. Let me say first, I haven't been watching any porn as I'm sure you'd know because…"

"Because I haven't received any alerts," Grant said laughing.

"Ha, ha. But I have been thinking about it…when we have sex. It's been very hard to separate it, not to think about it." Grant was taken back by what his wife just said. He moved his arm from around her and sat up. She didn't want to keep going at this point. She said, "I knew you were going to look at me differently."

"Steph cut me some slack. I'm just saying, here I think you're into me, but when we're having sex, I'm not the one you're thinking about."

"Grant, you'll never understand because this isn't what you battle, but if you research it as I have, you'll understand how porn changes your brain and how it functions. I didn't think I could talk to you about it to where you would understand without your ego getting hurt."

"My ego? Are you serious?"

"You see, that right there."

"What?"

"Your ego, pride."

"I knew this wasn't going to last long."

"So, what you sayin'?"

"You know how to mess up and a good time." Grant stood up and started putting back on his clothes, then said, "Let's go. If this is how it's going to be, then we can do this at home."

"So, is this what happens when I share my flaw with you? You run? Did you not just say if I can't talk to you, then who can I talk to? Would it satisfy you if I didn't talk to you about this at all and talk to some other man about it?"

"You did not just say that? Are you crazy or just stupid?"

"You know what, you're right, let's just go home. I can't believe I took off work for this!"

Grant, realizing what he just said to his wife, grabbed her by the arm when she tried to walk off and hugged her and said, "I'm so sorry, sweetheart. I never should have said that. I let pride get in the way. I'm sorry. Come on, I'm ready to hear the rest of what you have to say." He sat on the bed, and she sat on his lap.

"I don't know, Grant."

"Come on, babe. Please. I'm listening."

Stephanie exhaled and continued, "I try not to think about it when we are having sex, but sometimes, I can't help it."

"Can I ask you a question?"

"Yes."

"Is there a certain move I do that reminds you of a scene, or does it happen at a particular time when we're having sex?"

"I use it at times when I'm tired, but I want to give you me, so I need a jump start, and when you perform certain moves, it does trigger those thoughts, but I love it, and it feels good."

"Sweetheart, when you're tired, just tell me."

"But I'm tired all the time. After work, I just want to sleep, and I can't keep doing that. You have needs too."

"Yes, I do, but babe, as long as you're using that as a jumpstart, then you're not giving me you anyway. I want you, all of you. I want to be what turns you on."

"I get that, but should it matter how I'm turned on?"

"Are you convicted when you do it?'

"Sometimes, but most of the time, no."

"Could it be that you're not because the conviction is no longer powerful enough to penetrate the power you hold over it?"

"Okay then, Big Poppa!"

"Baby, bae-bay!"

"Oh my gawd! You so crazy."

"Aye, you started it."

"I know but anyways, you broke that all the way down. But I never thought about it like that."

"Maybe you should. If it's something you felt you needed to share, then it seems to be something you're not entirely comfortable with."

"I guess not."

"What is the testimony?"

"This time, when we made love, I didn't have a thought about any porn. It was just you and me."

"Did you hear what you just said?"

"What?"

"You said it was just you and me. That's the way it should be. When you have those thoughts, it's not just you and me. You invited something else into our sex life and made it a threesome. Another person doesn't have to physically be in our bed for it to be a threesome. God never designed it that way." Stephanie sat quietly listening to the wisdom of her husband. She realized he was right. "I don't think about another woman or any other woman I've slept with because my sole purpose is to please and satisfy you. You are the one on my mind. Steph (he kisses her on the lips), you are my world (he kisses her on the lips again with a little more umph). When we lay down (he kisses her on the neck), all I think about (he kisses her on the other side of her neck) is you." With that said, Grant dug into his repertoire and did some different things with Stephanie. He laid her down and kissed her, and once again, they were in the middle of the bed, making love. This time was different because she inadvertently taught Grant that he can't be the same way all the time; he has to switch it up. Later that night, they went out for a night on the town, then rounded up the weekend and headed home.

Chapter Fifteen: Is God Listening?

Grant came home from work one day and saw his wife zonked out on the couch with her work clothes still on. He walked into their bedroom, closed the door, and fell to his knees.

He said, "God, are you listening? Have you heard the prayers we have before You? I tell Steph to have faith, but mine is wavering. It's been over a year, and I still haven't heard anything from You. My wife is exhausted. I can't see her like this anymore. It's too much. Father, please show me something. Give me a sign, please." As soon as he got up from his knees, a call came in from his spiritual father from Savannah. Grant answered the phone and said, "Hey, dad."

"How are you, son?"

"A little frustrated."

"About what?"

"Steph and I have some things before the Lord. It's been a while now, and we still haven't heard anything from Him. It's been over a year. We've fasted and prayed. We've been studying the word together. We've kept the faith and continued to work while waiting on an answer."

"His grace is sufficient."

"I get that, but nothing? I see my wife and what she goes through every day. She asks me if God has given me an answer, and I have to keep telling her no. What does that say to her?"

"It says she trusts that you are before the Lord. Don't be frustrated, son. Don't lose hope. Don't lose faith. God is going to come through. I believe that. He has much in store for you all. I don't know what you have before Him, but He's going to come through."

"Yes, sir."

"Let me tell you why I called."

"Yes, sir."

"I have been laboring before the Lord myself, asking for help in the ministry. I have asked him to show me who will help this ministry grow and who can I mentor. He showed me you a few months ago, and every time I go back to him in prayer, He always shows me you and your wife. I know it's a big move, but He showed me how you guys have been praying together, studying His word even though time hasn't permitted it much. He sees your dedication. I want to offer you a full-time ministry position as my Assistant. Your title would be Pastor's Assistant. It will require you to be with me wherever I go. I will train you, and you will teach, preach, and lead in my absence. We will relocate you and give you a salary. It isn't a lot of pay starting off but will increase yearly. I want you to pray about it and talk it over with your wife."

"Wow, dad! I'm humbled. Although, I am surprised at Assistant Pastor."

"Why?"

"I mean, I've only been serving as a deacon at my church."

"God looks at the heart. He's seen you and your wife's labor. The doors God is opening for y'all...I can't even tell it all. I am also asking for you two to be over the marriage ministry. Y'all have a powerful testimony and married folk needs to hear it."

"Us? Marriage ministry? We're just getting footing. I don't know about that one. We still need to sit under some good teaching before taking over that platform. Yes, we have a good testimony, but it's a whole different animal teaching and running a marriage ministry. Maybe in a few years, but as of right now, I don't see that part."

"I understand. You see, that's honesty and maturity; something that is lacking in our church. Sad to say."

"Yes, it is, but I'm not squeaky clean neither. I still have a lot of growing to do. And I know this is a little off the subject, but what you don't know is this call looks like one of the answers to our prayers. I will talk with Steph and get back with you."

"Alright, son."

"Thanks, dad."

Grant hung up the phone, looked up to God, and smiled. He immediately went to wake up Stephanie. "Babe, wake up. Wake up."

Stephanie popped up and said, "Oh my God! 6:00? I'm late for work." She ran around the apartment, getting her keys to leave. Grant grabbed and her and said, "Steph! Steph! What you mean you late for work?"

"It's 6:00! I gotta go."

"It's 6:00 pm."

She stopped, looked around, and came to herself, then she said, "I was wondering why it was bright outside. It's never light out when I leave for work."

Grant laughed and said, "Babe, you are exhausted."

"Man! You don't know the half. They work me like a Hebrew slave. I'm gone need them to let My people go."

Grant laughed and said, "Well, hey, I got some good news."

"I could use some."

"I just got a call, and I believe with all my heart, it's an answer to one of our prayers."

"Cool. Who was the call from?"

"Pastor Garnett."

"How is he doing?"

"Good. He wants me to come and work by his side in the ministry and get mentored full-time."

"Full-time? What about your work?"

"That will be my work. I will see about getting my old job back as well, at least part-time. But Pastor said they will pay to relocate us, and I will receive a salary. All we have to do is pray to see if this is the direction in which God wants us to go."

"Hey, after today, I'm down for anything at this point. Let's pray, but it seems like you are already packed."

"It agrees with my spirit. We have been faithful despite it all. God is putting me into position. I know my purpose, and this just feels right."

Stephanie immediately thought about what God showed her about representing her husband and him being in position once she did what she was supposed to do and what God required of her. She worked on building her relationship with the Father, and now her husband is going forth. She couldn't have been more pleased. They prayed about it and received confirmation. Grant and Stephanie are headed back to Savannah in the next few months.

They were obedient to the instructions God gave them. They saved enough money to purchase a home in Savannah. Stephanie put in her notice right away, wasting no time after receiving the confirmation and her supervisor wasn't happy. He loved her work and tried to double her pay. She told him that she thought there wasn't enough money in the budget, and he came up with some weak excuse to make his earlier statements legitimate. That's when Stephanie realized he was using her to overwork her. He could get double the work done with half the pay. She gladly declined his offer.

Grant and Stephanie drove back and forth to Savannah to find a house and to look for a job for Stephanie. She wasn't having any luck, but then again, she wasn't worried about it. She was exhausted from the work she'd put in over the years and needed a break. Grant agreed. She still sent her resume to restaurants in the meantime. Grant mentioned to her about opening her own restaurant once they got settled. She gave it some thought and figured this may be a good time but wasn't sure. Meanwhile, she did look around, searching for a place to open her restaurant, planned out all the logistics, and created an album with pictures of what she wanted it to look like.

Stephanie's body was relieved of all the stress. She felt better. She was able to serve better because she was better. It took a minute for her to adjust, but she did it. Stephanie was sleeping all the time. When she first stopped working, she slept the day away every day. Grant would come home from work and see her sleeping on the couch. He knew her body needed the rest. There were days he'd pick her up off the couch and carry her to the bed and place the comforter over her. After a while, her body adjusted, and she wasn't sleeping as much. She'd work on things for the move.

On the other hand, Grant was very excited about moving back to Savannah but worried about who he'd bump into since he's still working on the documentary independently. He put it down for a while but picked it back up. He was scared about the "Ashley" situation. He got in touch with his old job and wondered if he could join the team again but only part-time. They allowed it. They knew to have him back on the team would be profitable in the long run. This documentary was important to Grant as well as finding the cure for autism since his little sister that was killed suffered from autism.

Their love life blossomed into something neither one of them could have ever thought imaginable. Stephanie learned it was just as Grant taught her years ago in that hotel room. She finally discovered what it is to give herself entirely over to her husband. There is a difference. Sex shouldn't be meaningless; it should be fulfillment. They were making up for lost times. After Stephanie left the restaurant, they were on top of each other all the time. Neither one of them had complaints.

One evening, Grant came home from work. Stephanie cooked dinner. She made oysters, asparagus, a cup of sliced watermelons, and a glass of red wine. He was ready to eat. Stephanie put in a movie, and they sat on the floor to eat dinner.

"This looks good, Steph," Grant said.

"I hope you like it," she said.

"You haven't cooked a bad meal yet."

"Awh…stop."

"I'm serious. My baby got skills."

"Thanks, babe."

"What all you do today?"

"Other than cooking? Nothing much. How was work?"

"It was good. I'm glad to be returning to the documentary."

"What stopped the documentary in the first place."

"I couldn't stay in Savannah any longer without my wife. I had to go, and the documentary at the time could not follow."

"What happened to Ashley? She put a lot of time and effort into the documentary."

"Yes, but she understood."

"I'd be mad with you."

He laughed and said, "Why would you say that?"

"Because all the work she put into it, just for you to bell."

"Hey, a brother had to do what a brother had to do."

"I guess."

"You not going to eat any oysters, Steph?"

"No, I don't like them."

"For real? Why did you make them then?"

"Because you like them."

"Come on, try one, just for me."

"Naw Grant, I'm cool. Just looking at it makes me want to vomit."

"Please…try just one." She said okay, and as soon as it slithered down her throat, she ran to the bathroom and vomited it all out. It made her shutter. It was disgusting!

She came back into the living room and said, "I told you I didn't like them. Now, look what you made me do."

"I'm sorry, babe," Grant said, laughing.

"It's not funny."

"Here, eat some watermelons." Stephanie ate some watermelons to try to get that oyster taste out of her mouth, but every time she thought about it, she ran to the bathroom. Grant put up the dinner and told Stephanie to just get in the bed. She said, "I'm alright."

"You sure?"

"Yeah, I'm good."

"How about we watch T.V. in the bedroom. I just want to chill." They did just that. Grant got a shower, and Stephanie brushed her teeth and got a shower too. They got into bed and watched a chick flick. It's not usually their flavor, but it was for this night. Later that night, when they fell asleep, Grant was awakened by hearing a noise coming from the bathroom.

"Steph, are you alright?"

"No. I think them oysters did a number on me."

"Are you allergic to them?"

"Not as I know of."

"Come on, let's take you to the hospital."

"I'm okay. I don't think it's that serious."

"If you are still sick, then that means something else is going on."

"I believe I know what that is," Stephanie said as she walked out of the bathroom with something in her hand.

"What's that?" Grant asked. She handed him the object, and he asked, "What does this mean?"

She said, "It means I'm pregnant."

"Huh? Wait a minute…how long have you…?"

"Have you noticed I haven't eaten much and I'm tired all the time, and when I do eat something, it doesn't stay down?

"Yes, but I thought that was because your body was tired from working at that restaurant."

"Are you not happy about it?"

"No, quite the opposite, I'm good! I just didn't expect that."

"I'm going to have to make a doctor's appointment to confirm it, though."

"You done let my seed get all up in that."

"Eww, nasty."

"You're having my baby," said Grant as he picked her up and hugged her.

"Please don't' twirl me around."

"Can I lay you down then?"

"That's how we go into this situation."

"Don't worry, I'll be gentle. I just got to have you."

Grant couldn't wait to tell his mom and brothers, and his colleagues about his big news, but he had to wait until they got it confirmed by a doctor. After the doctor's confirmation, he called and told his mother the very same day. He called Pastor Garnett. He wanted to call his in-laws but figured he'd give Stephanie a chance to tell her parents. She called her parents in the evening since her dad works during the day. It was hard for them to hold their excitement, but she held it until evening came, and both parents were home.

"Hey, pumpkin," Mr. Chase said, answering the phone.

"Hey, daddy. Is mama there?" Stephanie asked.

"Yes, you want to talk to her?" Mr. Chase asked.

"Put on the speakerphone. I have something to tell the both of you." Mrs. Chase came to the phone and said, "Hey baby, how's mama's girl?"

"I'm good, mama. Okay, I got you both on the phone because we need to discuss something."

"What is it?" Mrs. Chase asked.

"It's about Grant and me."

"What's the problem?" Mr. Chase asked.

"Here's the situation. We were trying to figure out the best way to tell y'all that you're going to be grandparents." Stephanie said.

"Well, the first thing you…wait…what!" Mr. Chase said.

"Y'all are going to be grandparents," Grant yelled.

"Oh, my God! Yes!" yelled Mrs. Chase.

"Congratulations, guys!" said Mr. Chase.

"And now that y'all are moving back home, we get to spoil our grandbaby every day," said Mrs. Chase.

They weren't counting on having a baby when they were focusing on moving. Having a baby hadn't even entered their minds. Nevertheless, they made the necessary changes to make the move more conducive. They only had a month before leaving to head to Savannah to live.

The time came for them to move. They said good-bye to good 'ole Jacksonville and all its woes. They moved into their two-bedroom one level home. It was newly constructed with a huge backyard. Grant hit the ground running with his new position. Stephanie worked in the ministry, heading up the hospitality auxiliary and sitting under the 1st Lady, learning from her.

Stephanie was glad to be home with her parents. She got to see them daily, and they even came to visit the church where they were serving. They had Sunday dinners at her parents just like old times. She traded porn for purpose, and it was more fulfilling. It doesn't mean she hasn't had struggles, but it does mean she took the necessary steps to overcome them. The enemy presented her with opportunities from time to time, but that's when she went to her husband and let him know her inward struggle. He kept her accountable and helped her through it. She didn't try to battle it by herself because she knew if she did, her flesh would fail her. This is what she wanted the show "Gem of a Lady" to portray. It doesn't show a woman who has it all together but a woman striving to get there. The Proverbs 31 woman isn't perfect. She knows who she is and what she is meant to do. God doesn't require something from us that we cannot do; He gives us what we can do, and that is His expectation. Now, her husband is known in the gates among the elders of the land, and he, along with their children, wake up and call her blessed. Their marriage isn't perfect, but they are perfect for each other. Porn doesn't have a hold over her any longer. She is free. It has no dominion over her. It's no longer a thought because she retrained her brain by covering her mind with the Word of God. She walks in His word, speaks His word, lives His word, and shares His word, which gives her a powerful mindset and gives her power over porn.

If you want to know about the side stories and what happened with the pregnancy, the restaurant, and the documentary, tune into their IG page named Grant & Stephanie and check our YouTube page.

About the Author

Keisha Lapsley

keycitypro@gmail.com

www.authorklap.com

Books

Homeless: My Favorite Park Bench

Homeless 2: Stained Worship (Coming Soon)

Homeless 3: Withered Flowers (Coming Soon)

A Love Worth Waiting For (Coming Soon)

Who Said Love Doesn't Hurt?

Jesus the Janitor

My Own Book of Psalms

The Gift of Helps: Learning When to Say NO!

No Mo' Explainin'!

I Did It Wrong!

My Writing Belongs to Him (male/female version)

Mentor Writing Courses

Self-pace Webinar

Keys to Writing 6-week Online Course

Keys to Writing VIP Upgrade Online Course

KeyCity Enterprise is looking for actors for upcoming web series and television shows.

Please submit all resumes and links to reels to keycitypro@gmail.com